She'd dreamed about Nick and a baby....

The baby had looked as good in his arms as a designer gown on a supermodel. They'd accessorized each other. Cute big dark head of hair, cute little dark head of hair. Broad shoulders, tiny fingers. Red tie, blue sleepsuit. The man and the infant had belonged together like apple pie and ice cream, like tulips and springtime, like baseball and hot dogs.

Cecelia's multimillionaire boss had held the little boy in a way that had made both man and baby look oddly vulnerable, so that both of them had tugged at her heart in a way she didn't want at all.

And she certainly never thought of her boss in a personal context like this. It was a point of professional pride to her that in seven years as an executive assistant for a total of six increasingly successful men in three different jobs, she'd never even come close to falling for her employer.

And I'm not falling for him now.

Dear Reader,

If you can't beat the summer heat then join it! Come warm your heart with the latest from Silhouette Romance.

In *Her Second-Chance Man* (SR #1726) Cara Colter enchants us again with the tale of a former ugly duckling who gets a second chance with the man of her dreams—if only she can convince him to soften his hardened heart. Don't miss this delightful story of love and miracles!

Meet *Cinderella's Sweet-Talking Marine* (SR #1727) in the newest book in Cathie Linz's MEN OF HONOR miniseries. This sexy soldier promised to take care of his friend's sister, and he plans to do just that, even if it means *marrying* the single mom. A hero's devotion to his country—and his woman—has never been sweeter!

Talk about a fantasy come to life! Rescued by the handsomest Native American rancher this heroine has ever seen definitely makes up for taking a wrong turn somewhere in Montana. Find out if her love will be enough to turn this bachelor into a husband in *Callie's Cowboy* (SR #1728) by Madeline Baker.

Lilian Darcy brings us the latest SOULMATES title with *The Boss's Baby Surprise* (SR #1729). Dreams of her handsome boss are not that strange for this dedicated executive assistant. But seeing the confirmed bachelor with a *baby?* She doesn't believe it...until her dreams begin to come true!

We hope you enjoy the tender stories in this month's lineup!

Mavis C. Allen
Associate Senior Editor

Please address questions and book requests to:
Silhouette Reader Service
U.S.: 3010 Walden Ave., P.O. Box 1325, Buffalo, NY 14269
Canadian: P.O. Box 609, Fort Erie, Ont. L2A 5X3

The Boss's Baby Surprise

LILIAN DARCY

Soulmates

SILHOUETTE *Romance*®

Published by Silhouette Books

America's Publisher of Contemporary Romance

SILHOUETTE BOOKS

ISBN 0-373-19729-2

THE BOSS'S BABY SURPRISE

Copyright © 2004 by Melissa Benyon

This edition published by arrangement with Harlequin Books S.A.

Visit Silhouette Books at www.eHarlequin.com

Printed in U.S.A.

LILIAN DARCY

has written over fifty books for Silhouette Romance and Harlequin Mills & Boon Medical Romance (Prescription Romance). Her first book for Silhouette appeared on the Waldenbooks Series Romance Bestsellers list, and she's hoping readers go on responding strongly to her work. Happily married with four active children and a very patient cat, she enjoys keeping busy and could probably fill several more lifetimes with the things she likes to do—including cooking, gardening, quilting, drawing and traveling. She currently lives in Australia but travels to the United States as often as possible to visit family. Lilian loves to hear from readers. You can write to her at P.O. Box 381, Hackensack NJ 07602 or e-mail her at lildarcy@austarmetro.com.au.

June 10, 1904

Dearest Mama,

This will be my last letter to you before your much-anticipated visit. I must confess I am counting the days, as I am getting so heavy and already feeling the heat. I am sitting in my favorite room as I write this, and I cannot wait for you to see it—well, the whole house, too. Frederick has worked so hard to make it perfect.

I spend so many happy hours here in my sewing parlor, looking onto the street. I have just finished making dear Cousin Lucy's wedding gown, a summer hat for me and Jemima's christening robe, as well as all sorts of pretty things for the baby, of course. I sit here in the afternoons and listen for my dearest Frederick to come home, and my thoughts fly all over the place. Mama, I never imagined I could be so content!

Sometimes I think that even a hundred years from now, my spirit will live on in this room, sending out hope and happiness and perhaps just a little mischief.

Your loving daughter,

Charlotte

Chapter One

One of the best things about flying business class, if you were an organized, efficient executive assistant like Cecilia Rankin, was that it was located right up at the front of the plane. There were no long, narrow aisles to negotiate, and no obstacle course of fellow travelers to apologize to as you eased your way past.

Stepping aboard the New York to Columbus flight in Nick Delaney's wake, Celie's fingers already itched to open her laptop, and she wasn't surprised when her boss himself picked up a conversation they'd abandoned midsentence a few minutes earlier, cut off by the boarding announcement.

"In fact, don't even get out the Fadden McElroy file," he said, stopping beside his seat.

"No, they didn't seem to have a grasp of the Delaney's ethos, I felt," Celie answered. The Delaney's chain of steak houses had recently fired its advertising agency, and this two-day trip to New York had been part of the process of selecting a new one. Celie had found it fascinating, though tiring.

"Exactly," Nick said, in answer to her comment. "The other agency presentations I want to review in-flight, but I'll make that call to the Chicago office, first."

"They'll want cell phones switched off soon," she reminded him.

"It's a quick call."

He pulled his cell phone from his pocket, flipped it open and keyed in the number. His strong body almost managed to fill the wide business-class aisle. Celie and Nick had been nearly the last passengers to board, and the flight attendants were beginning to make their final checks. Nick looked down at his seat as he spoke into the phone. There was a blue pillow on the seat, and he picked it up with a preoccupied expression, then stood back for Celie to pass.

As she took her seat, she debated removing the pillow from his grasp, but he had it tucked into the crook of his arm like a baby, and he was listening intently to the voice at the other end of the phone right now. She didn't want to distract him, even though she was sure he didn't really want the pillow.

It reminded her of something, suddenly, and she blinked. A baby. Nick and a baby. Nick and a baby that he didn't really want.

She'd dreamed this. Something very akin to this. The night before they'd left Columbus for New York, two days ago.

Celie lived in a cozy apartment in a big old house in the Columbus, Ohio, neighborhood of Victorian Village. It was a place that she sometimes felt might be *too* cozy, and too dangerously romantic, for an efficient, organized person such as herself, and she'd certainly never before had the vivid dreams she'd been having since she moved into it two months ago.

And this week, she'd dreamed about Nick and a baby. She could remember it in detail, now.

The baby had looked as good in his arms as a designer gown on a supermodel. They'd accessorized each other, so to speak. Cute big dark head of hair, cute little dark head of hair. Broad shoulders, tiny fingers. Red tie, blue sleepsuit. White shirt that was coming untucked, and a blue flannel blanket, also untucked. The man and the infant belonged together like apple pie and ice cream, like tulips and springtime, like baseball and hotdogs.

Celie's multimillionaire boss had held the little boy in a way that had made both man and baby look oddly vulnerable, so that both of them had tugged at her heart in a way she didn't want at all, and wasn't used to. He'd seemed different in the dream, not like the Nick Delaney she knew so well from the hours she spent in the same office with him. That Nick was confident, driven and impressive in every way.

In contrast, the dream Nick had had a softness to his eyes that had looked partly like fatigue and partly like tenderness, and both qualities had called forth an almost painful hunger inside the Celie-in-the-dream to go up to him, real close, lean into his tall, well-muscled body, lift her fingers to his face and—

Celie frowned and sat up straighter.

She didn't like having such vivid dreams, nor did she like remembering them in such detail. She was practical, responsible, efficient and in control. She wasn't a visionary. And she certainly never thought of her boss in a personal context like this. It was a point of professional pride to her that in seven years as an executive assistant for a total of six increasingly successful men in three different jobs, she'd never even come close to falling for her employer.

And I'm not falling for him now.

This employer, in particular, she sensed, would be a dangerous man to care for. He organized his emotions the same way he organized his life—in separate compartments, with strict labels. Celie valued this quality in a boss, but she didn't think she'd want it in a lover.

Still on the phone, Nick paced back and forth, the way Celie's sister's husband, Alex, sometimes paced back and forth when he was trying to soothe their crying baby girl. Little Lizzie had recently celebrated her three-month birthday with a weeklong visit from Kentucky to Columbus with her parents, and her aunt Celie adored her.

"Maybe I got Alex and Nick mixed up in the dream," Celie muttered to herself, as she opened her laptop.

"You okay?" he said, with his hand over the phone.

"I'm fine."

Nick saw that she had her laptop out. "Bring up the spreadsheets from Hampton Finn Lloyd, would you?"

He continued to pace. This was his caged-lion look, and he did it a lot, although today his movements were confined to a smaller area than usual. To and fro he went, like a big cat, with every muscle coiled, as if he had too much energy at his disposal to expend on a mere telephone call.

He would have to sit down, soon. The flight attendants had begun to close the aircraft doors. Celie managed to take the blue pillow from him, at last, in a deft maneuver that didn't disrupt his train of thought, the way her sister would take Lizzie from Alex, sometimes.

Nick didn't have any babies in his life that Celie knew of. Not one of his own, and no nieces and nephews, either. His only brother, Sam, although married, was childless. And if Nick was dating anyone, Celie didn't know. He wasn't the kind of boss who asked his assistant to buy gifts—or kiss-offs—for his girlfriends.

If she'd had to guess, Celie would have said he was uninvolved, right now.

Which means he's available, said a sneaky little voice inside her head.

She frowned at the voice, and mentally argued it down. For the second time in as many minutes.

Sure, she liked Nick. Respected him. Was aware of the powerful impression he made on almost everyone he met, with his clear gaze, his strong handshake, his quick mind. She even felt a little possessive toward him at times, running so many important aspects of his life the way she did.

Professionally, they accessorized each other, so to speak. Like baseball and hotdogs. Like tulips and springtime.

But all of this was a long way from feeling, like Celie-in-the-dream, as if she wanted to reach up and—

"Okay, now, these figures here," Nick said.

"Cost breakdowns on their proposed print ad campaign," Celie answered at once, happy to snap off that other, much more disturbing train of thought and focus on work.

The airplane engines began to speed up, ready to taxi away from the gate. The flight attendants launched into their safety announcement. Nick and Celie were forced to pause briefly during takeoff, when laptop and briefcase had to be stowed beneath their seats, but apart from that, Nick was as tireless as ever.

Only toward the end of the flight did he announce, "Okay, we'll leave it there. I'm going to call Sam."

"Do you want me to—?"

He shook his head, pulled out the phone again, and hit the speed dial. His eyes looked clouded, which they hadn't a few minutes ago, and his mouth looked a little tight. Celie had become adept at picking up Nick's emotional signals over the past eight months.

He was worried about his younger brother, the way Celie herself often worried about her mom.

He probably didn't realize he let it show, but Celie could tell, and she wasn't surprised. Sam was only eleven months younger than Nick, and she knew they'd always been close—close enough to make a spectacular success of working together for the past ten years. Sam's marriage had been in trouble, in recent months, and her boss didn't want his brother to get hurt.

"Where are you?" Nick asked him at once. "Home? Anything to report?" He listened for a minute, then told Sam, "No, just checking in. You on your own? Eating out?" He listened again, then added a little too casually, "Maybe I'll drop by."

In contrast to the casual manner, his eyes looked serious, focused and very blue. Actually, they were almost the same shade of blue as the airline pillow and the baby blanket in Celie's dream, she realized. The fact unsettled her again. Was that why she'd suddenly remembered the dream? Baby blankets, baby-blue eyes, his daddy's blue—

No. Surely not.

I'm just tired.

The flight landed on time, their bags were waiting for them on the carousel, and Nick's personal driver Leo whisked them away from the airport in Nick's personal limo within minutes. Since her apartment was almost on the route to his home in Upper Arlington, Nick dropped her there as usual.

"You look wiped," he told her. He wasn't being unkind, she understood, he was just making a statement of fact. His gaze flicked over her, taking in the creases in her knee-length charcoal-gray skirt, and around her eyes and mouth.

Her nerve endings heated under his regard in an unexpected way, and she nodded, feeling awkward. "Yes, I am," she answered. "It's good to be home."

"Take the morning off, okay? Come in at around two. If you need longer, just call and let me know."

"I'll be fine. Two o'clock."

"You sure?"

"We have the regional figures to go through," she reminded him. "And meetings to prepare for."

"We do. Okay, then. Two o'clock it is. Have a good night."

Leo had already opened the trunk to collect her bags and carry them to the door for her. Nick watched as Celie followed the older man to the side door that led up to her apartment. She had a straight back, a tidy walk, a taste for very efficient and very tailored professional clothing, and glossy dark hair that would have bounced in time to her footsteps if it hadn't been so neatly twisted and clipped high on her head.

Something moved in the corner of his vision. A curtain in one of the Victorian mansion's six apartments, maybe, wafting in the night breeze. Nick's muscles tingled with a sudden urge to chase after Celie and snap the clip off her hair so that its clean, silky bounce would become fact instead of imagination.

He resisted the urge, disturbed by how unexpected and how strong it was. He could almost feel her hair in his fingers. He kept watching as she reached her door, just ahead of Leo. Typically, she had her key already in her hand.

Of course she did. He would have been surprised if she hadn't, and Celie Rankin almost never surprised him. This was one of the things he liked about her.

She wouldn't let Leo bring her bags up the stairs, and disappeared inside within seconds. Leo headed back to the car, while Nick kept watching the big old house. A series of lights came on, showing Celie's progress up the stairs. Finally, the big, round turret room at the front of the second floor lit up. He saw a faint shadow through the drapes as she moved across the room.

Celie was a great executive assistant. Nick had kept her up until well after midnight in his hotel suite last night, working on her laptop, and he suspected her mind had been buzzing too fast afterward to wind down and permit her some good rest. No wonder she seemed tired, and a little offline.

He never had that problem. He'd learned very early in his life the trick of switching off and disappearing deep into the haven of sleep. As a young child, sleep was the only place in his life where he'd felt safe. Now his facility for deep, unbroken sleep allowed him to function at a higher level than many people during his waking hours, and he rarely remembered his dreams.

"Okay, Leo," he told his driver, dismissing Cecilia Rankin from his mind. He picked up his cell phone. "I'm going to call for some takeout and bring it over to Sam's, since he hasn't eaten yet. Can we swing by the Green Dragon, next?"

"I'm glad you're back," Celie's creaky-floored old apartment seemed to say to her.

The chandelier in the middle of the turret room's ceiling sparkled, and when she opened a window, a cool evening breeze wafted in. The antique clock on the side table by the door clacked like a percussionist playing out a rhythm. Eight o'clock, it read. Time to eat, her stomach said.

No problem, there. As efficient at home as she was at work, she kept the refrigerator in her little kitchen well-stocked with quick-to-prepare meals. Toss some frozen cheese ravioli into a pot of boiling water, heat a creamy pasta sauce in the microwave, tear up a few lettuce leaves, and she could eat in ten minutes.

Celie caught sight of her cherry-red robe hanging on a hook in the bathroom, and into her mind jumped the idea of taking a quick shower while the ravioli cooked, then eating in the robe and her matching slippers.

As a child, she'd been allowed to do that, when she was tired. Her mother would bundle her up on the couch with a crocheted blanket over her knees and a little tray table, spread with a linen place mat. She would eat a big bowl of homemade soup and fresh hot biscuits, and she'd feel so deliciously cosseted and safe.

She hadn't done anything like that for years. Since her dad's death, when Celie was seventeen, she had had to be the adult, the responsible one, the one who did the cosseting. It had seemed to frighten her mom if the daughter she depended upon displayed any sign of softness or vulnerability.

''You're exhausted. Baby yourself a little tonight, Celie,'' the robe on its hook seemed to say, but she ignored it and stayed in her clothes, afraid that if she gave in to the impulse she might fall asleep on the couch with the ravioli still boiling on the stove and not wake up until the kitchen caught fire.

She ate her meal, prepared for bed and fell asleep before ten.

The sound of a baby crying came to her ears after several hours of good rest. It seemed so close that it startled her awake. Or— But, no, was she awake? She found herself at the window, although she didn't quite remember how she'd gotten there. Had she walked? Or floated? Someone whispered a sound. Soothing the baby? Or calling her name?

The cries still came. In this room? They sounded close enough, but no. She looked around. There was no baby here. Outside, then? Downstairs?

The sound seemed distinct and real—as real as sounds and senses could feel in a dream, heightened more than they were in daily life.

Celie pushed the curtain aside and looked out. She'd kept the window open, as the April night was mild. The street looked quiet. She couldn't see anyone. Maybe the crying came from the apartment below. It sounded a little fainter to her ears, now. The couple downstairs didn't have a baby of their own, but they could have visitors staying with them.

She stepped back, and was about to let the curtain fall back into place when something on the windowsill gleamed in the moonlight and caught her attention. She picked it up. It was a hat pin, old-fashioned, with a long shaft of dull, dark gray metal and a big glass pearl at one end.

And that means I'm definitely dreaming, she realized, as part of the dream. *Because I've never seen this before.*

The glass pearl was pretty, and she imagined a dark-haired young woman with a wide, mobile mouth and friendly eyes, standing in front of a mirror and reaching her hands up behind her head as she used the hat pin to fasten a broad-brimmed creation of straw and chiffon into place on her thick pile of hair.

"This is a very nice dream," she told the woman. "If only that little baby would stop crying."

"Nick will go to him and soothe him back to sleep," the woman said. Her smile at once began to calm Celie's concern.

And a few seconds later, the baby stopped crying, so the woman pinning her hat must have been right. Nick had picked him up. Of course he had! Celie could see him with that little dark head settled on his broad shoulder and brushing against his clean-shaven cheek. His shirttail had escaped from his waistband again, but he was too absorbed in the baby to notice. Everything was fine.

Celie tucked herself back into bed with a smile on her face.

In the morning, however, the hat pin still lay there on her windowsill, and that was distinctly strange.

Dressed in her blue-striped flannel pajamas and only just out of bed, she picked it up and twirled its metal stem in her fingers as if the glass pearl was a little flower. So pretty, the way it caught the morning light. It made her think of Victorian lace, hand-stitched fabrics, elaborate hats and porcelain figurines. Despite its spiky point, it felt feminine.

When she thought about it, there was a perfectly rational explanation for its presence on her windowsill, too.

No, okay, not *perfectly* rational.

She wished she could find a better one.

But it was plausible, if you were prepared to stretch. The attic apartment directly above this one was in the process of renovation. The construction team had really torn into the place, pulling up floorboards and ripping ancient plaster off the walls. The hat pin must have gotten lost a hundred years ago, fallen through a crack in the floorboards and—

Well, here it was on the windowsill, so something like that had obviously happened, even if Celie couldn't quite picture the physics of it, right now.

And the baby—Nick's baby, protected in his strong arms—had been purely a dream.

For some reason, Celie didn't want to risk losing the wandering hat pin again, so she put it in the little zippered compartment on the side of her purse. After her usual light breakfast, she went to the mall.

"Sorry I'm late," Celie said breathlessly, as she entered Nick's office.

He looked at his watch.

She was right.

She was late.

By a whole two minutes.

And she looked a little different. Fresh, energetic, happy and well-rested, for a start, although he felt there was more to it than that. Her hair looked extra silky, and the clips had to be new. He didn't think she usually wore clips decorated with little flowers. They went some way toward undercutting the severe styling of her skirt, he thought, as did the pastel top she wore.

She definitely looked different.

This fact niggled at him a little, although he didn't have time to work out why. They had a lot to get through this afternoon. He allocated only a few seconds to the topic, and told her sincerely, "You look very nice."

She nodded, and said, "Thanks," and he knew she wouldn't expect him to pursue the question any further than that.

"Let's get right to those regional figures," he told her.

With various interruptions, the regional figures took most of the afternoon, and didn't leave Celie much time to contemplate her slightly disturbing morning at the mall. In the few moments she did have in which to think about it, she felt churned up inside. On the one hand, fluttery in the stomach, like a child going to a birthday party, but on the other, ill at ease.

At the mall, she'd kept thinking about her dream last night and about the hat pin. She'd even gotten it out of her purse a couple of times, to prove to herself that it was real...although she might have felt more reassured if it hadn't been. She'd been twirling it in her hand when the hairstylist had asked her, "Just a trim?"

And she'd felt the strongest temptation to answer, "No, I'd like to try something completely new."

She'd resisted it in the end. There was a good reason she always kept her hair up and out of the way. With the hairstylist waiting, and the hat pin still twirling in her fingers, Celie had needed several seconds to remember what the reason was—that it wasn't very efficient to have hair in her face when she was focused on work—but it did come to her in the end, and she opted for the usual trim.

She and Nick got through the regional figures by the anticipated time, and her boss was happy. When Celie got home that night and opened the closet to hang up two of the new, more softly styled tops she'd bought this morning to pair with her skirts—she'd worn the third top to work—the closet seemed to approve.

Several hours later, the bed wasn't so friendly. Tonight's dreams clattered into her mind with more violence, and the images were harder to put together. A figure lay on the floor of the kitchen. Her kitchen? The room looked familiar, and so did the figure itself, but then her dream lurched off into a different direction, she heard the sound of tearing fabric, and lost the image of the figure in the kitchen before she could decide exactly who it was, and what was going on.

The baby started crying, and she sat up in bed, alert at once, but the woman by the mirror told her again, "It's all right. Nick will go to him. Nick will care for him."

"I hope so," Celie answered. "But what about the woman on the floor?"

"Call her in the morning."

"Okay. Yes, that's what I'll do. Of course." The suggestion made so much sense that it soothed her back into sleep...or out of her dream...and it didn't occur to her that she didn't know *who* she was supposed to call.

In the morning, she woke late. Hurrying to prepare for work, she knew her sleep had been cut through by another dream, but didn't have time to try and bring it back to mind.

That happened later.

Sam's personal assistant, Kyla, told her, as they sat waiting for a meeting, "I love your hair like that. Any reason?"

"Oh, I just didn't get a chance to put it up this morning, that's all." She'd tried a couple of times, but for some reason her fingers wouldn't go through the familiar maneuver, and the fold of hair kept slipping sideways. In the end, she'd let it drop around her shoulders, still sheened and slippery from yesterday's salon conditioning treatment.

"You should wear it that way more often," Kyla said.

White-blond Kyla wore lots of jewelry, and lots of black. She was a single mother with a five-year-old daughter, Nettie, and although she came across as a ditz sometimes, she got things done. Sam depended on her more than Kyla herself ever let the man guess.

"I would, only it's not very practical," Celie answered.

She had that churned up, self-conscious sensation again. Somehow, she didn't feel quite safe. She suddenly remembered last night's dreams, and the reassuring advice of the woman who stood by the mirror.

"I'm supposed to call someone," she said aloud. "Check on someone."

She stood up in a panic, and it came to her in a rush. That figure, lying on a kitchen floor, wearing a nightdress and with one leg stuck out strangely...

Mom.

Eleven years ago, Celie's older sister, Veronica, had already been away at college when their father died, and her mom hadn't coped with Veronica's absence or with widowhood and grief too well. Celie herself had gone to college at Ohio State, so that she could remain at home. She'd moved into an apartment of her own several years ago, but still she never wanted to let her mother down. She spent a lot of time at Mom's, helping her out, and this morning's call to her seemed urgent, now.

A cluster of senior Delaney's executives and regional managers entered the room at this moment, carrying briefcases and sheafs of papers. Nick and Sam wouldn't be far behind.

"If they're ready to start, Kyla," she gabbled. "Tell them...uh...that I won't be long. Or—could you take notes for my Mr. D, if he needs it?"

"Sure. What's up? You look—"

"Nothing. I'm sure everything's fine."

Celie hurried to her private office, adjacent to Nick's, and keyed in her mother's phone number, but her mom didn't pick up, and neither did the machine.

Celie's mother had had a bone-density scan a few months ago, and the result had come back low. She took risks, too—vague, thoughtless ones that she didn't even realize were risks until Celie pointed it out. She went down the basement stairs of her little house without turning on the light. She put a step stool on the grass in the yard to reach up and prune a branch.

Celie had the phone number of her mom's neighbor Mrs. Pascoe in her address book, and she'd called a couple of times in the past to ask Mrs. Pascoe to check next door.

"Sure I'll go across, honey," Mrs. Pascoe told her today. "Just don't you worry, okay?"

But when Mrs. Pascoe called Celie back a few minutes later, her voice sounded very different.

"Thank heaven you called me when you did, Cecilia!"

Her mother had fallen from her step stool two hours ago while trying to change a lightbulb in the kitchen. She'd broken her leg, and she hadn't been able to get to the phone.

"I've already called 911," Mrs. Pascoe told her. "The ambulance is on its way."

Celie hung on the line, shaky and hardly able to breathe, and it seemed like an hour before the other woman came back to the phone again to report, "She's going to be okay, although the paramedics say it looks like a bad break. They've just left, and they're taking her to Riverside. You can probably hear the sirens in the background. She's in shock, after lying on that cold floor for so long."

Mrs. Pascoe hung up, but Celie's fingers were curled tightly around the phone and she couldn't seem to let it go. Nick appeared in the doorway while the receiver still hung in her hand.

"Kyla said—" Nick stopped, midsentence. "Heck, what's wrong, Celie? You've gone white."

"My mother's broken her leg. She had to lie in pain on the kitchen floor for two hours, with no help on its way. I dreamed about it. Which is just so weird.''

''You dreamed your mother broke her leg?''

''Yes. I saw a figure lying on a floor, only I didn't know who it was. Someone in the dream told me, 'Call her in the morning.' I remembered the dream just now, so I did call her, and when I did…'' She took a shuddery breath. ''Thank heaven I called!''

''Celie, it's all right. Keep remembering to breathe, okay? Are you going to faint?''

''No.'' She'd never fainted in her life, and didn't intend to start now.

''Help is with her now, right?''

''She's in the ambulance.''

''So it's okay. And for heaven's sake, don't worry about a little thing like a dream!''

''No. Of course. You're right.''

Celie felt herself sway. She didn't think she would have fainted, since she never had before and was so determined not to, but when Nick's arms came around her for support, strong and warm, she clung on to her boss for dear life and whispered hoarsely, ''Don't let go.''

Chapter Two

"We should get back to work," Nick muttered, after a couple of minutes—or maybe a couple of lifetimes.

Celie felt a little firmer in his arms, now, thank heaven, and a little firmer on her feet. He was no longer afraid she might just crumple into a heap on the floor, as he'd been a minute ago. She'd seemed completely boneless, as if she wasn't quite real, as if a formless wraith had invaded her body. He loosened his arms cautiously, and was relieved when she didn't crumple against him.

Still, he was reluctant to let her go.

She felt amazingly good.

Too good.

And different.

Surprising.

He didn't want an executive assistant who surprised him, and yet every sense told him that this was good. She felt far softer than she looked in her crisp

suits. Warmer, too. As warm as if he'd just climbed
into bed with her on a winter morning, or as if she'd
been toasting herself in front of an open fire moments
earlier.

As for the way she smelled... Faintly rose-scented,
like soap and shampoo lingering on clean skin and
hair. There were some other scents in there, too, but
he couldn't pick them. Good scents. Spring scents.
Classic. Not astringent and artificial, but soft.

His face had never lingered this close to her neck
before. Who knew that his efficient, unsurprising and
utterly reliable executive assistant would feel and
smell so warm and soft and sweet in his arms?

Nick let her go at last, stepped back and looked at
her, still standing close. She had a fuzzy look around
her gray-blue eyes and a new fullness to her mouth,
which changed her whole face.

He'd never considered that there might be this side
to Celie. Somehow, if he ever broke his own rules
and thought about her private life or the deepest emotions of her heart, he always assumed a level of...
safety, or something. Secretarial efficiency, even in
her heart. Neatly packaged emotions. Cautious affec-
tions. Suitable, unthreatening relationships.

After her first month in the job, he'd congratulated
himself on getting such a great assistant, and he'd
been determined to do everything he could to keep
her. She'd probably marry eventually, he'd calculated. Some local man, with a local career. He wanted
her still here at Delaney's when she had pictures of
her grandchildren on her desk, her hair still pulled
back in its efficient knot, but gray.

He'd always thought her intelligent, capable and
practical, but he'd never considered that she might be

a deeply passionate person as well. He wondered if she knew this about herself. It seemed possible that she didn't. So new to him, the hint of this unsuspected passion around her eyes and mouth stirred him to an extent that shocked him, and tilted his balance. He didn't like it, and he definitely didn't want it to upset the status quo.

She smiled at him carefully. "Getting there," she said.

He could almost sense the way her blood beat in her veins. Her hands were clenched into fists at her sides, and her breathing went in and out steady and strong, as if she had to work hard to get it to happen at all.

I'm watching her body, he realized.

He was watching the way her lower lip had dropped open, and the way her breasts moved when she breathed. In eight months he'd never thought about her breasts. Her suits tended to tailor them out of visible existence, but the softer top she wore today above her straight navy skirt hugged her shape much more closely. He couldn't tear his eyes away, even though he knew it wasn't right.

In another second she would notice, and of course she wasn't thinking about anything like that. She was thinking about her mother, and her disturbing, clairvoyant dream.

Nick didn't believe in psychic dreams, himself. He'd learned early on to believe only in the things he could see and touch and feel for himself. His adoptive parents were practical, rational people who'd worked very hard to rescue him and Sam from the darkness of their early years, and he had enormous respect for their attitude.

His dad had retired a few years ago, and they wintered in Florida, now, so he saw less of them. He still felt they were close, however, and still shared many of their beliefs. Even those he didn't share, he respected.

From the beginning, his mom and dad had encouraged their boys to respond to the tangible proof of their care—things like home-cooked meals and bedtime stories—and not to go stirring up the murky memories that lay beneath, by reading anything into the bad dreams they'd sometimes had.

No, like Mom and Dad, he definitely didn't believe in the significance of dreams.

But he could see how upset Celie was, both by what had happened and by the fact that she thought her dream had warned her of it in advance. Of course she was upset!

"Sit," he urged her, emotional himself, worried about her, thrown off balance. "I'm going to ask Kyla to get you some hot tea and something from the cafeteria. Then we'll talk about how much time you'll need. Your mother's here in Columbus, right?"

"Yes. In Clintonville. They're taking her to Riverside." She didn't sit, she just stood there, leaning her left hand heavily on her desk. Her fingers splayed out fine and neat and long.

"What would you like to eat?"

"Oh, I…I'm not really hungry." She waved away the idea of food with a graceful right hand that looked limp with shock.

"No, you should," he urged again. "Even just a muffin."

"Okay, a muffin."

"Because I'm not letting you drive like this."

"Drive?"

"Don't you want to try and see her before she goes into surgery?"

Her face cleared, leaving her brow wide and smooth, and bracketed softly by the hair she'd left loose this morning. "Yes, of course. Oh, could I? Can you spare me right away? Can Kyla handle the rest of the meeting? I have the files laid out on—"

"Don't worry about it, Celie. Between us, we'll manage. Take as much time as you need. A couple of weeks, if you have to."

"Thank you, Mr. Delaney!" She smiled again.

Celie had a gorgeous smile. He'd noticed it very early on, when she'd just started working for him, and he remembered thinking it was such a huge professional asset it was a shame she couldn't list it on her resume. Today, the smile was wide and soft and wobbly, far more heartfelt than he'd ever seen it look before. She couldn't keep it in place, and it faded at once.

"Please save the Mr. Delaney stuff for executive meetings," he said. "I'm just Nick. How many times have I told you that?"

He took her arm, led her to her ergonomic chair and pushed her gently into it, then called Kyla from the phone on Celie's desk because he didn't quite trust what his executive assistant would do if he left her alone, even for a moment. If she thought she had to clear her desk, leave memos, check her e-mail before she departed… It would be typical of her to think that.

"You're still a lot shakier than you realize," he told her.

"No, I'm not," Celie answered. She added more

firmly, in order to clear the ambiguity, "I mean, I do realize. How shaky I am. Now. Thanks. The tea will help."

She watched Nick take the tea and a blueberry muffin from Kyla a few minutes later. "Thank you," he said. He clicked his tongue at Sam's assistant, curled his fingers around the disposable cup and cradled the paper muffin plate in the opposite palm.

Something had happened just now. She and Nick hadn't kissed, hadn't come close to that, but it was the most potent *hug* that Celie had ever experienced. She could still feel Nick's body against hers, and smell his scent—clean male, mixed with professional laundry—on her skin. She could feel the throb of secret places inside her.

He'd felt so solid and strong and steady, and she'd needed that, after the shock of the prescient dream and her mother's pain. She'd made no attempt to let him go, even when her dizzying weakness began to ebb.

And then he'd told her she was free to go to her mother right away. She'd never needed time off at short notice before, and wouldn't necessarily have expected such care from him. She knew how driven he was. A lot of men as successful as he was would have been far more ruthless with their staff's personal time. It turned out he didn't have total tunnel vision, however.

She remembered how she'd let her head rest against his chest, listening to his breathing and his heart, and how she'd wrapped her arms around him as close and tight as they would reach. She'd felt the prickle of his belt buckle against her stomach, and the squashy nudge of her breasts against his ribs. While

it was happening, she'd felt too shocked about her
mom to react as a woman, but as she relived the moment now, in a slightly calmer state, her skin began
to tingle.

"Okay. So," Nick said. "Do you need extra cash?
I'll write you a check."

"I don't need it, Nick," she answered. "I just need
the time. You're giving me that, and I'm grateful."

"Don't come back too soon."

"No, I won't. Thank you again. So much."

"Don't worry about it. Just take care of your
mom."

Celie didn't see Nick for a week.

She barely saw her apartment, either, as her mom
needed a lot of time, at first in the hospital and then
at home. After a week, her mom still wasn't too confident on her crutches, but by this time Celie's sister,
Veronica, had organized to come up from Kentucky,
with baby Lizzie, for as long as she was needed,
which meant that Celie could go home and back to
work.

The apartment sent out its silent "Good to see
you" message, the moment she walked through the
door. The clock on the side table had stopped, the air
was a little stale and surfaces needed dusting. On the
windowsill, Celie found a torn shred of white broderie
anglaise fabric, left there like a message on a Post-It
note.

A message for her.

She had no doubt of that.

But where had it come from, who could have put
it there, and what did it mean?

"Hey, what's going on here? Why are you doing

this to me? I'm not the right person for it,'' she said aloud to the room, and when she turned, she almost expected to see the woman fixing her hat in front of the mirror, wearing a broderie anglaise blouse.

But no one was there.

I'm talking to my apartment, she realized. *How weird is that?*

At least the solution to this problem was obvious, and within her control.

Don't do it.

Celie hadn't had any memorable dreams while at her mom's, but tonight they again cut through her sleep. The baby cried. Or was it a doll? She kept seeing strange figures and forms, some of them reassuringly like people, others just the suggestion of a human shape. What were they made of? Plaster? Metal? None of the images stayed long enough for her to identify them. Bright lights flashed, startling and dazzling her, and she thought there must have been an explosion.

Where was the baby in all of this? Was it in danger?

She jumped out of bed and rushed to look for it.

No, not it.

Him.

Nick's baby was a boy. Hadn't the woman in front of the mirror said so, last week? Celie sniffed the air, in search of the acrid, firecracker smell of explosives but, thank goodness, couldn't detect it anywhere.

Couldn't find the baby, either. His cries still shrilled in her ears. Why didn't Nick go to him tonight? His inaction distressed her. The baby was his. The woman had implied it, and Celie somehow knew it herself, in any case.

The baby belonged to Nick, only tonight Nick didn't seem to be around.

"He doesn't know," she told the woman frantically. "Nick doesn't know the baby's crying. He doesn't know about the baby at all."

"He will," she answered, with the calm smile that made Celie feel as if everything was all right. "He'll find out. You can tell him, if you want."

"And the explosion?"

"It's not an explosion. The baby is miles from there, anyhow, on the other side of town. No one's in that kind of danger."

And this meant that Celie could sleep, so she did. This was very easy, because of course she'd been asleep all along. None of this was real.

In the morning, it felt great to be back at work, and even better to be busy—back the way life used to be, in this job, very safe and structured and efficient, with no time to think of Nick Delaney as anything except Celie's driven, demanding employer. She wore her severest navy pinstripe suit and rocketed through the tasks Nick had given her with barely a pause to sip her coffee.

He had scheduled a long day. Meetings and conference calls ran until five, ahead of tomorrow's demonstration of proposed new menu items by the resident team of Delaney's food scientists and chefs. Delaney's rotated its menu seasonally, four times a year, and although Ohio was currently clothed in spring colors, the new offerings for the coming fall were already in planning.

Celie wasn't surprised, midafternoon, when Nick

announced, "I'm going to go visit a couple of the restaurants tonight, check out the atmosphere."

Nine years ago, there had only been one Delaney's, and Nick and Sam had been able to check out the atmosphere in that establishment for sixteen hours of every day. Now, with ninety-eight existing locations and twelve more planned to open this year, the chain was so large and so successful that they risked losing touch with the ambiance they'd worked so hard to build. It must be more than seven years, Celie guessed, since Nick had personally thrown a steak on a Delaney's grill, or poured a Delaney's beer.

"You want to take notes?" she asked him. "You want me to come along?"

"I'd like you to come along. I don't know if we'll need to take notes. I just want to get the feel. Sam's doing the same with Kyla, over near his place, at Delaney's Franklin Street."

Nick didn't mention Sam's gorgeous red-haired wife, Marisa. He rarely did, these days, and Celie had always gotten the impression that he didn't like her. Celie had trouble with the woman's snobbish attitude and social climbing instincts, herself.

They left Delaney's company headquarters at just after five, and drove to Delaney's Mill Run in Nick's very average-looking American car instead of the chauffeur-driven limo, with Nick himself at the wheel. Celie suspected that he kept the car especially for times like this. He hated to be recognized as co-owner of the corporation when he dropped in at one of the restaurants. Getting any kind of special treatment would defeat the whole point of the exercise.

A perky college student showed them to a booth in

the bar section, and as Nick had hoped, she had no idea who he was.

Although it was only midweek, the place already had a Friday-night mood, with groups and couples laughing and talking over appetizers, cocktails and beer. The decor was fresh and clean, and diners could choose booths or tables, lounge chairs or bar stools. In towns and cities all across America, Delaney's was the kind of place where a man could bring a woman, confident that she would like the atmosphere and he would like the beer.

Up in a high corner across from their booth, a big television showed news and sports, but it didn't dominate. Nick took a seat with his back to it, and didn't even spare it a glance. Celie knew what he must be thinking. How many people in here? What was the gender balance? The age mix? The ethnicity? How many people ate in the bar section, and how many had one drink here, first, before moving to their table in the restaurant itself?

The Delaney's marketing division had facts like these at their fingertips, but Nick liked to sample the data in a more personal way. He and Sam both believed that this was the way to pick up on trends and apply them successfully.

"Who's watching the TV?" he asked Celie, when her club soda and his light beer had arrived. "I don't want to turn 'round and stare."

"Three guys. No, four. There's news coming on, now."

"TV in a bar is a real guy thing, isn't it? Figures show a significant difference in the demographics we get when the layout of the restaurant is—"

He stopped. Celie tried to smile, to encourage him

to go on by showing him that she was listening, but she couldn't. All at once, the image on the television screen had her vision and her concentration in a tight lock.

Reporters were jostling to get close to a politician so they could ask questions. Cameras flashed, lighting up the screen like explosions.

Camera flashes.

She'd seen camera flashes in her dream about Nick's baby in Cleveland last night. She'd interpreted them wrongly until this moment, but she knew they were significant all the same.

"Cleveland," she said aloud. The baby was in Cleveland.

She stood up automatically, as if the cameras were flashing in her own face and the reporters wanted to interview her, wanted to put her picture in the newspaper. Then she sat again, just as abruptly, as the strength drained from her legs. That message about Cleveland and Nick's baby was suddenly so clear— far more clear than she liked. She didn't want this to be happening to her. She wanted her life, and her subconscious, to stay just the way they were.

"Cleveland?" Nick asked. His voice came from far away, and he shot a quick look behind him, toward the television screen, following the direction of Celie's gaze. "No, that's Washington, D.C. Some political scandal. What's the matter, Celie?"

"I—had a dream last night, with cameras flashing in it," she answered, her gesture at the television as limp as a wet rag. "I didn't realize until now that that's what they were. I thought they were explosions. They mean something. They're important, somehow. And the dream has something to do with Cleveland."

Your baby is in Cleveland, Nick.

Should she tell him this?

Or would he think she was as crazy as she feared she might be?

"Well, we're going there next week." He frowned. "We have the art museum opening."

"That's right. I'd forgotten."

As part of its corporate philanthropy, Delaney's was sponsoring a major sculpture exhibition, which would be seen in only four U.S. cities during its world tour. Cleveland was one of them. Celie had been extensively involved in liaising with the Great Lakes Museum of Art during the planning stages of the tour, but most of the details had been finalized months ago.

With her mother's accident, she'd forgotten the opening was so close. Nick had meetings in Cleveland that day, and she'd already booked hotel rooms for an overnight stay after the event. She'd been looking forward to the glamorous occasion, and had bought a new dress—simple, black, appropriate but glamorous all the same. Now she wondered, with a sick, sinking feeling, if she ought to be dreading the evening instead.

"Hey, it's okay," Nick said. "Here take a sip of your drink. No, hang on..."

He slid out from his side of the booth and came to hers. Resting his upturned hand on the table, he coaxed her head forward and down so that his palm cradled her forehead. His other hand stroked the nape of her neck for a moment, then slid lower, to rest on her back.

"Take some deep breaths," he said. "Are you going to get sick?"

"No."

"When you can sit up, take a drink and then tell me what's wrong. This is the second time I've seen you like this in a week."

He stroked her back. His touch was firm enough that she could feel the weight and warmth of his hand, but light enough that it caressed her skin through the thin knit fabric of her top like running water. It wove a net of sensation all around her—a net that she could have cocooned herself in for the rest of her life.

When she sat up, a little too soon, his face blurred in her vision but she could still perceive the depth of his concern, and it disturbed her.

She'd never needed him in this way before, and now, as he'd said, it had happened twice in a week. She didn't want to need him, didn't want to have a *reason* to need him. She wanted her life fully under control, and she was sure he'd feel the same. They both took pride in their professional boundaries, and in how much they could handle on their own.

"It's okay," she told him. "I'm fine."

"Yeah, right," he drawled. "Sure you're fine." He brushed her hair behind her ear, touched her shoulder lightly, frowned at her. He narrowed his eyes, and his lips parted. Celie stared down, and heard the hiss of his breath, very close. "Are you still worried about your mother, Celie? Did you come back to work too soon? You look like you're falling apart."

"I keep having dreams with messages in them," she told him, pressing her hands together in her lap. "Last week, I dreamed about my mom breaking her leg. I have cameras flashing in my face as if they're telling me something. I hear your—I hear a baby crying, and the crying is a message."

"I'm not sure that I believe in dreams like that," Nick answered slowly. "In fact, I know I don't."

"I never used to, either." She looked up at him again and tried to smile. "Until I started having them. I don't want to believe in them. But how can I help it, when they come true? If you could talk me out of believing them, Nick, trust me, I'd be grateful."

She reached to pick up her glass, and gulped a mouthful of her drink. The dry fizz stung in her mouth. A loud burst of laughter came from a nearby booth, and a party of new arrivals trooped past to the group of low chairs in the far corner. Delaney's was filling up, and getting noisier.

"Let's get out of here," Nick said. "I want to put a good meal into you, and I want to talk about this. But not here, where I'm thinking about Delaney's and trends and the next advertising campaign. Let's go somewhere quiet, where nothing else is going to impinge."

Celie didn't argue.

Nick flung some cash on the table and they left immediately. Celie paid no attention to where they were going until he parked in front of one of the city's most exclusive restaurants. Salt was the kind of place where most people needed a reservation, even on a weeknight. Nick Delaney didn't, because unlike the college-student waitress at his own restaurant, the deferential maitre d' at this establishment knew at once exactly who he was.

"Better?" Nick said, as soon as they were seated.

Only a few tables were filled as yet, and the clientele was well-dressed and very well-behaved. So were the staff. The waiters skimmed back and forth on silent feet, and even the sounds that came occasionally from the kitchen were muted against a background of soft, smoky music.

With effort, Celie created a smile. ''Are you saying you don't like your own restaurants?''

''I love our restaurants. Tonight, this place seemed like a better idea. Somewhere more discreet, where we can relax. With staff who'll protect our privacy. I want to hear about the dreams, Celie.''

She told him about the image of her mother lying on the kitchen floor, and the image of cameras flashing, somehow telling her *Cleveland*. She didn't tell him what she knew about the crying baby yet, but she did tell him about the hat pin, the woman in front of the mirror and the scrap of torn broderie anglaise.

Since she still had the hat pin in her purse, she took it out and showed it to him.

''You're right. It has to be the renovations upstairs,'' Nick said. He ran a fingertip along the gray metal toward the point, and for half a second Celie could almost feel the touch of his finger on her own skin.

His confident tone reassured her, but she pushed at the issue, all the same. ''Renovations give people dreams that come true?''

''Renovations could give someone a hat pin on their windowsill.'' He looked up. ''Isn't that what you thought, yourself?''

''I'm not so sure, anymore.''

''And, yes, renovations are stressful and unsettling. People dream more when they're unsettled. The dreams themselves can be explained.''

''Then do it, Nick, please. I want explanations for this.''

"You were already concerned about your mother, right?"

"She's elderly. Her bones aren't strong, and she takes risks without thinking about them. I've been responsible for her since my father died, eleven years ago, and she's never regained the ground she lost when she lost him. Part of her just...*left*...and I've had to pick up the slack."

"You don't talk much about all that."

"There's no need. It's under control and it's not your concern. I love Mom, and I'm happy to help her. But, yes, I do worry."

"So there you go. Both your conscious and your subconscious mind feared an accident, and it happened."

"And the flashing cameras? What do they mean? Why are they saying Cleveland to me?"

"The exhibition opening next Tuesday night is a big deal. You know that. The press will be there. No surprise if we get cameras flashing in our faces. Subconsciously, you must be a little nervous about it."

Celie pretended that he'd convinced her. She wanted him to have convinced her, but he hadn't. Not really. The dreams remained too vivid in her mind for that. They threatened her own sense of who she was.

As she'd just told Nick she'd run her mother's life, and her own, from the age of seventeen. She didn't have a mystic, intuitive streak. She had responsibilities. She couldn't afford to have dreams that competed with reality in her mind.

Their waiter brought menus and they both ordered. Celie chose a fennel bisque soup and grilled chicken, while Nick decided on shrimp and beef. "Would you like some wine?" he asked.

"Just a glass."

Even one glass turned out to be a mistake. It loosened her tongue just that little bit more, and as they ate she found herself telling him, "There's another dream I've been having, too, Nick, repeated night after night. It makes even less sense than the others."

"More predictions? Do I want to hear this? I'm trying to help you get your feet back on the ground, Celie."

"Are you?"

"For the best of reasons. You're getting too stressed over this. It's eating at you more than it should. Look at the way you're frowning at me."

"You're right. I am." She squeezed out a smile and touched her forehead with her fingers, trying to smooth the frown away. "I—I don't know if the dream is a prediction. But it gets a little clearer, each time. Maybe you can tell me, because I do think that there's a message in it, and the message is for you."

She took a breath, and twirled the hat pin between her finger and thumb. Its rounded, pearly end gleamed in the leaping golden light from the candle in the center of their table. Nick's china-blue gaze was fixed on her face, and she felt as if she was swimming in the deep pools of his eyes.

"Tell me, Celie," he said. "Don't hedge it, or qualify it, just tell me."

"Okay, then, here it is. Is there any chance, Nick, that somewhere in this world—" *Cleveland, let's say* "—you have a baby you don't know about?"

"A *what?*" Nick almost yelled the words.

"A baby," Celie repeated.

She leaned forward and captured Nick's big, firm hand in hers without even realizing she'd done it. It felt warm and dry and strong—even stronger when he twisted it out of her grasp and closed his fingers over her knuckles. He squeezed them and looked down, drawing her attention to the body contact. "Pick up your spoon, Celie," he said.

"I'm sorry." She slid her hand away at once, and continued, "It's a little boy. I hear him crying, and I get up to go to him, and then there's a woman who tells me it's all right, I don't have to, because you'll go. And the crying stops, and I feel a sense of peace because I know you're there, holding him, belonging with him. Only last night, you didn't go."

"I...didn't...go."

"To the baby. And I realized it was because you didn't know that he exists. Believe me, as I've said, I'm not happy about these dreams, and I know this one sounds—"

"He doesn't exist, Celie. The dream is nonsense." He frowned. "Boy or girl, I've never fathered a child."

"But I'm wondering if that's true," she persisted, still caught in the strong, sticky web of the dreams, forgetting her allotted place in Nick Delaney's life, overlooking her own doubts. "You know, sometimes a woman gets pregnant and she has reasons for not wanting to tell the father. It happens. I don't want to trespass into your personal life, but if you think back, look through your diary, isn't there someone who could have gotten careless with—?"

"No." The flat of his hand came down hard on the table. "I'm telling you, it's not possible, Celie, and you need to believe me on this. I really hope you're not suggesting that I give you a list of the women I've slept with."

"No, of course not."

"And that I should call them up and ask?"

He looked angry now.

Of course he did! This whole conversation was an affront to his privacy, to the boundaries they both believed in and to their whole working relationship. Celie should have seen it, but even if she had, would the dreams have prompted too strongly for her to resist? She needed to understand what was going on.

Her fingers slipped, and the hat pin pricked the ball of her thumb, as if to taunt her, "Gee, didn't you handle this well?"

She dropped the hat pin on the table, beside the remains of her meal. She had no appetite left for it, now. The restaurant had filled, and the few couples who'd been here when she and Nick first arrived had reached coffee and dessert. If Nick didn't want to listen to this, then it was time to go.

"Just how long do you think such a list would be, if you don't mind my asking?" Nick said, his voice deceptively quiet and controlled, this time. His blue eyes sparked.

"I'm sorry," she answered quickly. "I thought I should tell you about what the dream seemed to be saying. That's all. Since it was so vivid. And so real. Of course I'm not suggesting you keep a—a list."

"But you're suggesting there'd be some names on it if I did? That there's a woman out there from my past—and this is an infant we're talking about, so you think it's my *recent* past—who's been pregnant with my child over this past year and I haven't known? That I could have been that careless, that casual, and not even thought to follow up on it?"

She gaped at him, her cheeks on fire. "I'm sorry,"

she said again. It sounded terrible when he said it like that. What was happening to her? How could a few dreams have taken such a strong hold on her imagination?

Their eyes met and held. His still shot flames of anger, making his strong face look even stronger. She straightened her spine and tried to gather some dignity, for both their sakes.

"I didn't intend to overstep the boundaries of my role," she said. "But obviously I have."

"You got that right," he growled. "I wouldn't have expected it of you, Celie."

"If you want my resignation, Mr. Delaney, you can have it first thing in the morning."

Chapter Three

Nick picked up the hat pin and flicked it between his fingers, like a baton twirler with a baton. He watched the bright color flare and flame in his executive assistant's cheeks. He could tell how badly she was beating herself up over her mistake, and realized how much of it was his own fault. He'd encouraged her to open up and talk about what was troubling her, and then he'd bitten her head off, just because she'd gone further than he'd wanted. His anger changed its focus.

"Of course you're not going to hand in your resignation, Cecilia Rankin," he told her impatiently. "There's no need for that."

Lose the best person he'd ever had in the job?

Not willingly!

Not over a momentary blip in their professional relationship like this one. The dreams couldn't mean what she thought they meant. He was certain of that. Without the minor coincidence of seeing cameras flashing on the television news, after she'd dreamed about the same thing the night before, and without Celie's subconscious concern for her mother echoing the heavy responsibility she took for her on a day-to-day level, he wouldn't even have needed to talk her out of this. She'd have seen it as rationally as he did.

"All right," she said, her tone careful. "I'd rather stay. I do know that I'm of value to you."

"But you are going to get your feet back on solid ground, okay? You haven't been quite yourself just lately. I definitely haven't fathered a child. If I ever marry, it'll be a very well-thought-out step with the right kind of person, and we'll look long and hard at the issue of becoming parents before we take that step. I've always been incredibly careful to make sure that fatherhood wouldn't happen to me by accident, and it hasn't."

The antique hat pin stilled between his fingers and he looked down at its iridescent, pearly end.

"And that's a blessing, if you want the truth," he added, his voice dropping. "Because I'm not sure that with my background I'd be remotely good at it."

"Right," he heard Celie say, in a different tone. "Okay. I'm sorry. I didn't know you felt that way."

Of course she didn't.

Even to himself, he'd never articulated the issue quite so starkly before. As he said it, however, and heard the echo of it in his mind like an instant replay in a televised sporting event, he knew it was true. He didn't see himself as a father. Not as a *good* father, and as he'd just told her, he wouldn't take on the role if there was any risk at all on that point.

"You know, when you've had a start in life like

mine and Sam's…'' He stopped, cleared his husky throat.

Hell, he didn't want to tell her any of this!

The strange thing was, he had virtually no memories of it, anymore. It was too long ago. He'd been too young. He just remembered that he'd had memories once. He'd done his best to get rid of them, considering that they made him vulnerable.

They were like nightmares, or like monsters. Hunger and violence. Neglect and loneliness. Fear and pain. Sessions of hide-and-seek with Sam, the two of them wedged in a…no, it was no good, he couldn't remember the detail…wedged in some precarious hiding place. Games that were anything but games.

"Do you know," he heard himself saying, "I only have one actual, clear, conscious memory left of my early childhood, before Sam and I were adopted."

Celie nodded slowly, her gray-blue eyes wide in a face that looked pale against her dark suit. He remembered that he'd told her he and Sam were adopted. Neither of them made any secret of that fact, but they never talked about what their lives had been like before.

The glint of the hat pin's glass pearl drew Nick's gaze downward again and he continued as he stared at it. "It's just one moment. Hardly even a memory. I'm opening a fridge door, and inside there's an ice-cream cake. Beautiful. I can still see it, as if it was yesterday. It had fairies on it, wearing pink ballet tutus."

"Not for a boy, then. Not for you or Sam."

"No, I guess not. It's not in the freezer part, and it's been there a while, because it's half-melted. I have no idea when this was. I have no idea why it was there. Someone's birthday? As you say, it probably wasn't mine or Sam's. Some kind of celebration? All I remember is a rush of mouthwatering greed, an aching pang in my hungry stomach and an urgent excitement about telling Sam so he could have some, too. There's food, Sam! And it looks good! And if we eat it quick enough, before someone comes, we might not be hungry again for a while!''

Ah, shoot!

He dropped the hat pin on his empty plate, and it seemed to clatter and chink as loudly as if he'd dropped a knife there instead. ''I really don't know why I'm telling you this,'' he said.

''Because it's important,'' she murmured.

''That's often a reason not to say it, don't you think? We hide what's important. The trivial stuff we lay out like a pack of cards.''

He looked up and saw her still watching him, with a serious, motionless mouth that he suddenly ached to kiss, now that he knew more about the real woman beyond the efficient facade. Such a lovely mouth. And kissing her would be such a delectable way to change the subject. He imagined her in his arms as he tasted those warm, beautiful lips.

Hell, what was he thinking?

Kissing her would be the perfect way to ruin an ideal professional relationship.

And telling her about his and Sam's questionable start in life wasn't a whole lot more sensible. He'd set the boundaries himself, now he wanted to break them? What had gotten into him?

''But I'm glad you did say it,'' Celie told him.

She brushed a stray strand of hair behind her ear. Lately, her hair didn't seem to want to stay in its neat clips the way it used to, and she often had to make the gesture. With her fingers tracing the outline of her ear, she looked as if she was listening to some distant echo.

"What about you?" he heard himself say. "Do you think you'll want kids someday?"

"I'd like to, if it's with the right person."

"Just like that?"

She smiled. "No, not just like that. I've thought about it. I'm not kidding myself that parenthood is easy, but then anything in life that's worthwhile is also a challenge."

"My parents are great," he told her, despite everything that told him he should shut off the flow right now. "My adoptive parents," he revised. "Only I never think of them that way. With the qualifier. The *adoptive* bit. They're just Mom and Dad, and they've been great from Day One. Sam and I must have been a lot of work for them, at the beginning."

"I guess you've never searched for your birth mother?"

Nick huffed out a short laugh. "Open up that can of worms? No."

"I didn't know you'd had such a hard time."

"Why should I talk about it? To you or to anyone. It's in the past. It hasn't affected who I am now."

But that wasn't true, Celie thought, as she watched him. It had had a huge effect on who he was now, even if he couldn't see it himself.

He twisted in his seat and said, with an impatience she was accustomed to, "I'd like some coffee. Where's our waiter? Okay, over there." Seconds later, he'd raised his arm and drawn the man's attention at once, with a quick nod and a smile.

Celie looked at his squared jaw, his honed physique, the evidence of his restless energy. She thought about Nick's protective attitude toward Sam, his need for boundaries, his dislike of mess and what he'd just told her about his feelings on fatherhood. If he really thought he carried no legacy from his first few years, he was wrong.

Tears pricked in her eyes, and she hoped he wouldn't see. The perfect executive assistant didn't cry when she thought about the brave, protective, determined, neglected little boy her boss must once have been. And no driven, multimillionaire boss wanted to discover that his assistant had learned so much about the man he was inside, from just a few short phrases and a single evocative anecdote.

Tonight had already been way too personal for both of them.

His dismissal of any possible truth to her baby dreams should have made Celie's belief in them crumple completely. And she should have been relieved about that because she didn't want to believe in the dreams, any more than he did.

Oddly, this hadn't happened. There was a place inside her that felt more certain on the subject now, despite all the scary implications that certainty brought. The baby couldn't be possible, couldn't be real, and yet belief hardened inside her like cooling taffy.

Somehow and somewhere, more than likely in Cleveland, Nick had a baby boy. Even if it wasn't biologically his, as he'd insisted so strongly it couldn't be, the baby belonged to him. The baby needed him.

Celie picked up the hat pin from Nick's empty

plate. She twirled it between her fingers, admiring, as always, the way its knob of pearly glass caught the light. As she put it back in her purse, something seemed to tell her that she should just let the whole subject of the baby and the dreams rest for a while.

Yes, no kidding! If I want to keep my job! she thought. *Not to mention my sanity.*

But she knew there was more to it than that.

Aside from the way the dreams threatened her own sense of who she was, this was about Nick himself.

He wasn't ready for his baby, yet.

"I don't believe in any of this, you know," Celie told the woman in the dream, several nights later.

"Neither does Nick," the woman answered.

Celie's show of defiance didn't seem to ruffle her a bit. She had an old-fashioned dressmaker's dummy in the room, and she calmly pinned the hem of a floor-length blue gown as she spoke, taking the pins from a puffy pincushion fastened to her wrist. The mirror reflected a warm, golden light.

"He's a little concerned," the woman added.

"I know that."

"Concerned about Sam, too."

"You see? You're not telling me anything I don't already know. Sam's marriage is in trouble. Nick knows. Kyla knows. We all know."

The seamstress just smiled and went on with her pinning. "Sam will be better off once she leaves," she said.

"Marisa?"

But the seamstress didn't answer because the baby started crying. This time Celie felt so certain that someone—a woman—was standing outside in the street with the baby in her arms looking for Nick, that she ran…floated…to the window to call down to her. "Wait!"

"She wanted to wait. She couldn't," said the seamstress, over Celie's shoulder, and when she looked into the street, no one was there.

Nick picked up the phone in his Cleveland hotel suite. He glanced at his watch as he waited for Celie's voice on the other end of the line. They'd cut the timing a little too fine, after today's meetings had run late. His room-service meal had been slow to arrive, and he wondered if she'd had the chance to eat.

She picked up, finally, sounding breathless, and he asked her, "Ready, Celie?"

"Can I meet you in the lobby? Leo will be waiting."

"Take your time."

"No, it's all right."

He guessed she was still finishing with her makeup and shoes, just across the corridor, but didn't push her to admit the fact. She never admitted to being caught on the hop. Or she hadn't, until recently. He'd always assumed she considered it part of her role as the perfect executive assistant. She probably had some kind of executive assistant manual with an instruction in it that read, "Never let your boss know if things aren't running right."

In the week since their far-too-personal dinner at Salt, she'd pulled back into her efficient shell, like a turtle hiding from danger. He'd been relieved at her distance, and grateful.

Thanks, Celie, he could have told her, for understanding that we both said a little too much to each other that night.

Tonight he wondered for the first time if there might be more to it than that, if her tactful silence was about protecting herself, as much as protecting her employer and the boundaries of their professional relationship.

Her retreat hadn't been total, he realized. There were subtle signs that their dinner together had changed her perception of their relationship, but he couldn't put his finger on them immediately, and didn't try to dig any deeper. The way she smiled? The way she held her body?

No, he definitely didn't want to think about it too much.

He took the elevator down to the lobby, and didn't encounter her on the way. She was right, Leo was already waiting out front with the limo. "Celie's going to be another couple of minutes," he told his driver.

He looked at his watch again. Since Delaney's was the exhibition's major sponsor for the Ohio section of its tour, they couldn't afford to be late. Celie and Nick were the corporation's public face tonight, as Sam had gone to the Caribbean this week with Marisa, at short notice, in an attempt to repair their rocky marriage. Nick paced around the lobby, too restless to sit, or to take his place in the limo. The elevator door pinged as it opened behind him. He turned and saw Celie coming toward him. Who would have ever guessed that she could look this good?

Her dress was very plain, just a black, figure-hugging sheath with narrow straps and only the smallest suggestion of cleavage, but her height, her grace, her figure and the color in her cheeks turned her from an executive employee appropriately dressed for a formal evening to a sensuous woman hiding her assets in plain sight.

As she drew nearer, he saw that she looked a little flustered, as if she'd indeed had to hurry to be ready in time. The pink cheeks and the wide eyes and the not-quite-perfect hair gave her something of that emotional look he'd seen in her recently, and he felt his blood begin to heat up in a way that had become all too familiar.

Professionally, he might wish she didn't have a life or a beating heart beyond her efficient facade. As a man, however, he was increasingly aware of how strongly he responded to this new side of her—the side he'd only recently begun to see.

He didn't believe in mixing business with pleasure. Who would have known he could be so tempted to break his own rule?

"We should get going," he said, his voice catching at the back of his throat.

"I'm sorry, my meal didn't arrive," she answered, then scraped her teeth lightly across her full lower lip. That mouth again. It pulled his gaze like a magnet.

"Same here."

"I only had time for a few bites."

"So you haven't eaten?" He touched her back, but took his hand away at once, as if the contact might burn them both.

"Not really," she said, half turning so that the light fell on her neck and shoulder. "It's fine. There's supper tonight, isn't there? I'll graze."

It shouldn't have sounded like a suggestive line, but to his ears it did.

The museum reception room and adjacent exhibition galleries were already crowded when they arrived. Cameras flashed, just the way Celie said they had flashed in her dream, and Nick felt her flinch beside him. He moved closer to her, took her arm and checked her face. Okay, she'd relaxed a little.

Northern Ohio dignitaries and socialites schmoozed with each other. A television news crew from a local station filmed the guests and the sculptures. Nick immediately plunged into the part of the evening he hadn't looked forward to.

He shook people's hands. He made small talk. He accepted the accolades he and Sam had earned by deciding to sponsor this major art event. These sculptures had been loaned from important art museums all over the world, and some of them were hundreds and even thousands of years old. Speeches began, and he listened to them, then made one of his own. Everyone applauded.

Then he saw Celie waiting for him with the glass of iced water he'd asked her to have ready, and his body told him that the whole evening was worthwhile just for the sake of seeing her looking like this, so tall and elegant, so cool on the surface, so unexpectedly emotional beneath. Fire, sheathed in ice.

"Do you have friends and relatives in Cleveland, Nick?" she asked him as he slaked his dry throat with the chilled water.

"Some business acquaintances," he answered. "More of them since we decided to do this art thing. I wouldn't call them friends. Not yet. Why?"

She smiled and gave a tiny shrug. "I just wondered. You obviously like Cleveland. This was where you and Sam chose to branch out first, after Columbus, and you still do so much test marketing here. You chose to support this art museum, rather than one closer to home.''

''I do like Cleveland,'' he answered. ''I like the lake, and I'm a rock-and-roll fan. The Rock and Roll Hall of Fame is pretty cool.''

Celie nodded at Nick's casual response to her question, but she wasn't satisfied with it.

Cleveland. Camera flashes. Nick's baby. She sensed a triangular connection just around a corner in her mind, just out of sight. Should she try and get beyond that corner, or stay safely where she was?

They wandered past the priceless sculptures, pausing side by side in front of reclining nudes, abstract glass shapes, bronze goddesses and marble figures of the Madonna and Child. The sleeve of Nick's tuxedo brushed her bare arm.

Since the opening night was so crowded, they had to stand closer than they usually did, and Celie couldn't decide which was harder on her growing awareness—to stand at a distance, where she could see just how impressive he looked in his tux, or to stand close like this, where she could feel his heat.

She took another sip of her wine, and wished she'd chosen club soda or orange juice, instead. The waiters with their trays of appetizers kept missing her and, on a near-empty stomach, she didn't want the drink to go to her head. She didn't trust herself anymore, in so many ways. Didn't trust her efficiency, or her control, and that meant she had to find new elements to rely on.

The dream woman in her apartment had suggested, in a cryptic, roundabout way, that Nick's baby was here in Cleveland, and Celie didn't know what to do about it.

Do nothing, the rational part of her said.

The rational part won—for now, at least—since she wasn't even sure that she wanted to let the other part of herself exist, let alone have a voice in her life.

"The baby looks weird, doesn't it?" Nick said.

It took Celie a moment to realize that he wasn't talking about *his* baby—the one he denied could even exist—but about the one right in front of them. The infant was carved in marble, and he had baby-soft contours and dimples, but the Renaissance sculptor had given him the proportions of an adult rather than a child.

"I like these classic sculptures, though," she answered. "They're stylized and formal, with the traditional poses, but if you look at their eyes and mouths, you can see the humanity, and the emotion."

She braved the vigilant museum guards and dared to reach out and touch the stone. It had a creamy, waxy look. Because of the richness of personality in the faces of the Madonna and Child, Celie almost expected the piece to feel warm. When her finger made contact, however, the illusion faded. The marble was cold.

"I guess you're right," Nick was saying. "Whoever modeled for this Madonna, or whichever real woman the sculptor was thinking of, probably had joys and sorrows much like ours, even though she lived five hundred years ago."

They talked about a whole lot of things, their heads bent close together so they could hear each other above the noise, until Celie discovered that she'd finished her drink, and that the crowd had begun to thin out. They must have let this conversation run on for quite a while.

"You should really talk to some more people," she reminded her boss, as the old, hyperprofessional Celie might have done.

"I'd rather leave," he said. He didn't need to stand so close anymore, and yet he didn't move away. "We've done what was expected of us."

"Your speech was nice." She touched his sleeve, and felt his fingers brush her wrist. They both let the contact drop, but the awareness remained. "You added a couple of bits after the draft I printed out."

"Thanks, they were an impulse and I wasn't sure they'd work."

"They did."

"I'll say good-night to a couple of people, then we'll go." He curved his hand lightly over her hip and around to the small of her back, then moved away. "Meet me by the exit, just there?"

He joined her a few minutes later, and she felt a dangerous rising of happiness inside her because they'd escaped the crowds, the camera flashes had stopped and it was just the two of them again.

I can't think about him this way, she told herself. *I know that.*

But she went on doing it, all the way back to the hotel in the limo, and up in the elevator, and along the corridor to her room, and when he stopped beside her, standing too close, as she fumbled in her evening bag for her plastic key card, she knew they were both in trouble.

"You usually have your key ready, Celie," he said softly.

"I—I forgot tonight."

"Why?"

"Because I—I—" She looked down at her glittering black bag, feeling helpless. Nick had leaned closer. "Because…"

"You don't have to say it," Nick told her.

"I'm tired, and I feel like something's happening, but—"

"Don't say anything. Don't. Just let me do this. Let me go with this."

He pushed lightly on her shoulder and pulled on her hip, pivoting her away from the door. Her hand dropped to her side, holding the forgotten bag that contained the elusive room key. His mouth brushed hers. Slow. Soft. Sweet.

Celie closed her eyes, lifted her face, parted her lips, wanting this in a way she couldn't remember ever having wanted anything before. And when he wrapped his arms around her and deepened the kiss, she felt as if the whole universe had suddenly held its breath.

Chapter Four

Nick had kissed a good few women in his life. With a couple of those women, he'd gone a lot further. But he'd been so careful never to pursue anyone who was for any reason out of bounds, unsuitable.

Kissing Celie, he couldn't even remember at first, why this wasn't in his game plan. She had no husband or fiancé or boyfriend in the picture. She had no financial interests in a rival restaurant chain. And right now, in his arms, she felt perfect.

His awareness of her swamped every sense. She smelled like fresh flowers. Her mouth felt like warm cake and tasted just as sweet. She moved against him like a mermaid swishing through water, rippling and sensual and strong. She even sounded good. What were those kittenish sounds she was making, as she plucked at his shirt hem?

Protests.

They were protests.

She was trying to tell him that she didn't want this,

although every strand of evidence in her body said something very different.

Lifting her hands to his face and cupping his jaw, she pushed harder, with a more serious intent, and their mouths parted, leaving him bereft.

"Is this a good idea, Nick?" she whispered. She stroked his hair back from his forehead, and let her soft palm slip down his cheek. She touched her mouth to his once more, printing the shape of her gorgeous lips there so that he knew he would sense them in his memory for months. He felt her breath feather his skin as she repeated, even more carefully, "In view of our successful working relationship, is this really a good idea?"

He groaned, and remembered why she was right. "No, it's not a good idea," he admitted. He'd had some crazy thought that kissing her might get his new awareness of her out of his system, so that their relationship could fit back where it belonged, but as soon as he'd touched her lips, he'd forgotten all about that.

"You're outside my hotel room door," she said. "It's after midnight. I didn't want to stop this…"

"But clearly I wasn't going to," he finished for her. "So you had no choice."

"Something like that. It seemed best." She stroked his face again, as if apologizing, and he knew that it wasn't fair to leave her in the position of watchdog over their conduct.

He stepped back, taking his share of the responsibility, already aching from the loss. Now that they weren't touching anymore he realized just how closely and hungrily she'd pressed her body against him. He took in the sight of her mouth, swollen from passion, her hair tumbling around her face and the dizzy look in her eyes. If he'd had any thought, at first, that she'd found it easier to call a halt to this than he had, he'd been wrong.

"Thank you for saying what I should have said," he told her. "More to the point, I shouldn't have let it happen at all, and I'm sorry."

"So am I."

"Do you have your key?"

"I'm looking for it right now." She rummaged through her purse, head lowered. He couldn't see her expression. "Here it is." Relief blew through her tone like a rush of wind.

He saw her fumble to get the key card into the slot, but he stood back and didn't help her, even when her first two attempts at sliding the card failed to trigger the lock. He didn't trust what might happen if he let himself touch her again, and he wasn't going to risk losing her professional input for the sake of one incandescent night.

Or more than one.

They'd already blurred their boundaries far too much, in recent weeks.

He'd spent the past six months, or more, witnessing the slow, inevitable meltdown of his brother's marriage because Sam had married the wrong woman for the wrong reasons. Nick had no desire to make the same mistake. Sam's current suffering confirmed Nick's decision to choose his involvements very carefully, whether those involvements were fleeting or serious.

His executive assistant wasn't on the list, in any category.

He heard a click and saw a tiny green light as the key card tripped the electronic mechanism at last. She leaned on the handle, pushed the door open and found the light switch just inside.

"Sleep well, Celie," he told her, his voice husky.

"Thanks. I'm tired. I should sleep."

But the smile she gave him was short and half-hearted and didn't reach her eyes. He had a pretty good idea that she wouldn't sleep a wink, and that for once, lying just across the corridor from her in his own suite, he'd be as wide-awake as she was.

Celie told herself that she wasn't going to feel uncomfortable about what had happened with Nick outside the door of her room. They'd both agreed it was a mistake, and a complication they didn't want. It had happened, they'd disposed of it, and she could forget about it now.

Easier said than done.

The two of them returned to Columbus first thing the next morning, opening laptops and spreading out papers in the back of the limo while Leo was still turning over the engine. They must both have looked very busy, but somehow, in spite of all the activity and the mess of papers, not a lot was achieved.

Celie decided the top and skirt she'd brought for today in her overnight bag were a mistake, particularly the lace edging at the sleeves. Lace and efficiency didn't mesh. She'd have to remember that, in future. Unexpected dangers confronted her when she stepped out from inside her efficient, professional shell.

Back at Delaney's corporate headquarters, Nick gave her a long list of tasks, then shut himself in his office for the rest of the day, communicating with her via terse e-mails and interoffice phone conversations that lacked his usual easy fluency. Celie made up her mind that this was all for the best. The awareness and the awkwardness would both fade if they were conscientious and careful. She'd make sure of it.

She would make sure her hair stayed up as neat as possible in its knot high on her head. Extra pins or clips should do the trick. She would choose her work wear from the suit-and-jacket end of her closet, and not get tempted by the softer, more feminine garments that she'd been buying over the past couple of weeks.

She would even take the hat pin out of her purse when she got home, because its suggestion of Victorian femininity and softness was obviously a bad influence on her state of mind.

Her apartment, unfortunately, didn't seem to agree with her decisions on any of this.

The weather had gotten colder overnight, and when Celie turned her key in the lock at just before six in the evening she discovered that the rooms were freezing. Investigating the old-fashioned metal radiators, she found that the valves were closed, although she was certain she hadn't left them that way. In the night, she dreamed that she was cold, and sat up in bed to find that her pretty quilt and matching sheet had slid onto the floor.

"Is this how you want it to be?" the seamstress said. She looked toasty warm, herself, with a pale gray Victorian velvet cape draped over her knee as she mended one of its seams. It looked downy soft and almost silver.

"Of course not!" Celie answered. Indignantly, she gathered the quilt and sheet back onto the bed. "Don't look so smug about it. I can see you're warm!"

"You could be, too, in his arms."

"And out of a job, in a few months, when it all

falls apart. Stop acting as if you have all the answers.''

''Nick won't risk falling apart. That's part of the problem. Show him the way people can change. Don't you want to?''

Celie wanted to ask the seamstress what all of this meant, but somehow she'd already lain down and pulled the quilt around herself again, and the warmth was stealing over her so thick and fast that it made her too sleepy to word the question. The next time she awoke—or the first time, because she couldn't really have been awake before—it was morning, and there on the windowsill she saw some threads of pale gray fabric.

Something was missing, though. It took her several minutes to work out what it was, and when she did, she didn't know whether to feel relieved or alarmed. For the first time since the seamstress had begun to appear in her dreams, the baby hadn't cried.

And since Nick had already told her that the baby couldn't be his, and couldn't even exist, maybe the dreams meant nothing after all.

Definitely they meant nothing.

Getting dressed for work in front of the mirror, she couldn't see anything special about it, despite the warm, pretty light that always seemed to reflect from it in her dreams. She chose a straight black skirt and a gray jacket to wear to Delaney's corporate headquarters. Gray could be a soft, warm color, in the right combination, but when teamed with a stiff white cotton blouse, it only looked cool and impersonal.

She added three extra pins to her hair, shook her head vigorously from side to side, and was pleased to find that everything stayed put...until she tripped over the edge of the rug and landed sideways on the bed, and it all fell down around one ear.

Re-neatened, so to speak, and on her way to work a little later, Celie felt angry with herself, with her own subconscious, with the seamstress in her dreams and with her entire apartment. She only narrowly resisted the urge to slam the door behind her.

''Nick Delaney's office,'' Celie said into the phone at two o'clock the next afternoon. It was Friday, and she felt ready for the weekend, ready for some distance. She'd defiantly worn her most efficient and least feminine brown-pinstriped trouser suit to work this morning, and felt uncomfortable in it—stiff and hot, even when she took off the jacket to leave only the cream silk top. She finished, ''Cecilia Rankin speaking.''

''I'd like to speak to Mr. Delaney,'' said a woman's voice.

''Could I have your name, please, and can I let him know what this is about?''

Uncertainty vibrated down the phone, like an electric current. ''It's a personal matter,'' the woman finally replied. ''My name is Ellen Davis, but that won't mean anything to him. I'm calling from Cleveland, which just might.'' Celie heard what could have been a sigh. ''Probably not, after so long,'' the stranger added.

''From Cleveland?''

It meant something to Celie.

If she believed in her dreams.

Did she?

With a hand that was suddenly clammy, she pressed the button for Nick's line and heard a distracted "Yep?" from him down the phone a few seconds later.

"I'm putting through a personal call for you, Nick," she told him.

"Can it wait, because I'm right in the middle of—"

No, it couldn't wait. She cut him off, midsentence, and left him in Ellen Davis's hands. She was half-convinced he'd storm out of his office a minute from now to yell at her for wasting his time by not adequately screening his calls.

The executive suite on the top floor of Delaney's corporate headquarters seemed very quiet this afternoon. Still in the Caribbean, Sam had told Kyla to take the afternoon off, unless anything urgent came up. No meetings were scheduled, after some talks with two executives from the corporation's new advertising agency this morning, and there were no tech support people around dealing with uncooperative computers or copy machines.

More silent than anyplace else was Nick's private office. With his door shut, Celie couldn't hear a sound, even though her own door was open. She tried to concentrate on the figures she was adding, but they blurred in front of her and made no sense. The total on her pocket calculator didn't match the total on the printout, and it should have done. Muttering under her breath, she pressed Clear and began again, narrowing her focus down to each digit and keying them in with total precision at a quarter of her usual speed.

The door to Nick's office opened twenty minutes later, just as she finished checking the figures. Her head flew up so fast to look at him when he appeared in her doorway that her neck bones crunched. Her stomach lurched at the sight of his face. It was so pale it looked green, and so ravaged with shock that she was surprised he could put one foot in front of the other.

"It's the baby, isn't it?" she blurted out, rising from behind her desk. Was this why she hadn't heard the sound of crying the past three nights? The woman with the baby who was looking for Nick had located him at last.

"How did you know?" He flicked a hand past the side of his head, impatient with the way he'd worded the question. "Yes, I know you dreamed about it. Which is weird enough. But how did you know that woman's phone call, just now, was about the baby? This whole thing is—"

"Because she said she was calling from Cleveland."

He nodded numbly, and explained, "She saw our photo in the Cleveland newspaper on Wednesday morning, taken at the exhibition opening on Tuesday night. She'd tracked me down a couple of weeks earlier, she said. She knew exactly who I was, but hadn't made contact. She had doubts about whether it was the right thing to do. But then she kept coming back to the photo, and something she saw in it convinced her that she should make the call."

"Something in the photo?"

"She was vague about exactly what."

He began to prowl Celie's office, doing his caged-lion impression, back and forth in erratic figure eights, and she watched him helplessly, a million thoughts jostling for space in her mind. For a start, she still expected his knees to buckle at any moment. That was how bad he looked, how totally shocked.

She wanted to get him to sit down, drink a glass of water. She wanted an explanation that filled in all the gaps and made sense. She wanted him to look happy, just a momentary smile, or something, so she'd know this was good news, and not a disaster.

Didn't a baby have to be good news?

"Tell me about the baby, Nick," she said, stepping closer. "Tell me it all."

"I want to go up there," he answered.

"To Cleveland? Now?"

"Yes, now. I'm useless for anything else today. I want to see this woman. I want to see this—my—this child."

"Leo's taking the ad agency people to the airport, then you told him he was free for the weekend," she reminded him.

"Do you have your car? Could you drop me home? I'll drive myself."

Celie took a breath. "I'm not letting you drive close on a hundred and fifty miles the way you look right now, Nick."

He blinked, and tried to squeeze the numbness out of his face, but it came right back.

"Sam and I have a sister, Celie. A half sister. Or we had," he corrected himself heavily. "She had cancer, but she wouldn't accept any treatment until her baby could be safely born, and by then it was too late. She started trying to track us down when she realized how ill she was, but then she had to pass the search over to Ellen, her foster mother."

"Ellen Davis. The woman who called."

"Ellen has the baby now. His name's Carter. He's five months old." He switched gear again, knocking her almost as far off balance as he clearly was himself. "Can you grab your keys?"

"I'm not letting you drive," Celie repeated.

She didn't know how he'd react to her confronting

him like this, but the issue was too important to let slide. He definitely didn't look fit to drive. She went up to him, desperate to offer some support, or even just some direction, but didn't know what to do. Hold him in her arms? They'd been so careful not to touch since Tuesday night.

He circled his fingers around her wrist and ran them up her arm. Every nerve ending in her body sprang to attention. "Come with me," he said. "Drive for me. You're right. I wouldn't trust myself at the wheel. I need to get my head around this, and fast."

"Let me grab my bag and switch off my computer."

"Go ahead," he invited her vaguely, but he didn't let her go. He was chafing her upper arm as if it was a piece of furniture he was sanding back. His eyes had darkened into opaque, glistening pools.

"Nick?" Celie reached around and closed her hand over his, successfully coaxing it loose from her arm. She had to fight to keep her breathing steady. "You could switch your computer off, too."

She touched his shoulder and his neck, above the collar of his silver-gray shirt, releasing an unexpected waft of the balsam-sweet shampoo he must have used this morning. Need began to pool deep inside her in a way that had become far too familiar, and she wanted to lean closer and wrap her arms around him.

She had to bite her lip and squeeze her fists together to resist the pull, but she knew that Nick himself was too distracted to feel it right now. She could almost hear his sharp mind racing, like a current zinging through his body.

"I'm glad you were here," he said, and at last she felt his strength and dynamism return. "What's the time?" he said. "Almost two-thirty?" He strode toward his office, while Celie turned to her desk. "We won't get there until five."

"Did you tell Mrs. Davis you were coming today?" she asked.

"Yes, and I have the directions to her house. She says she remembers me. Dear Lord! She could be anyone. There are people who'd try a scam like this. But she gave me details, and they all fit."

His big body in its charcoal suit looked cramped in the passenger seat of Celie's blue Ford compact, but if he was aware of this, he didn't let it show. They had a clear run out to I-71, and headed northeast while Nick gave out a clipped report on what he'd learned from Ellen Davis. The sudden control and distance in his tone troubled Celie. She preferred the emotion he'd shown back in her office.

"Mrs. Davis fostered Jane on and off for years, apparently, from when Jane was a baby," he said. "Our birth mother had some problems. She tried to keep all three of us, but she couldn't. I guess Sam and I would have been a handful. Eventually she realized it would be easier on everyone if she let us two go, and made a clean break, gave us a fresh start. I don't blame her for it. How can I, when Mom and Dad have been so great?"

"It must have been a very difficult sacrifice for her," Celie said.

"She never let go of Jane, though, and took care of her when she could. I can't understand why I don't remember a baby sister."

"You were how old, when she was born?"

"Almost three."

"Just a toddler, Nick. Of course you don't remember."

"When our birth mother wasn't functioning so

well, Mrs. Davis stepped in. Jané had her own troubles growing up, apparently, but she was so thrilled about the baby. She and Mrs. Davis talked about what should happen. Mrs. Davis is almost seventy, now. They decided to try and track Sam and me down, in the hope that one of us would be prepared to adopt.''

He stopped, and the obvious question burned on Celie's lips. Was he prepared to adopt his tiny nephew? She didn't dare to ask it. Not yet.

Instead, she watched the road. It was a beautiful afternoon. The brief cold snap had lifted again, and the temperature had to be around seventy degrees, with the sun shining bright in a blue sky. The rolling Ohio farmlands were clothed in the fresh spring-green of new corn, and wildflowers were beginning to come up between the two sides of the highway.

Nick moved in the seat beside her and she glanced across at him, but could hardly believe what she saw. He was getting out his laptop? She hadn't even taken in that he'd brought it with him.

''What are you doing?'' she blurted out. ''Work?''

''Crunching a few figures,'' he answered. She heard the click of the keys for several minutes, then he announced, ''The obvious thing to do is to set up a trust fund for Carter, and also to finance full-time professional in-home assistance for Mrs. Davis so that she can continue to care for him without compromising her own health. I'll run it past Sam, obviously, but I'm sure he'll agree with the plan.''

He sounded as if he was discussing the marketing strategy for Delaney's upcoming openings in California.

''But Mrs. Davis wants one of you to adopt,'' Celie said. She looked across at him again.

He keyed some more figures into the laptop, then

saved and closed the file he'd set up. "That's impractical," he answered. "Sam and Marisa's marriage is too rocky, and even if it wasn't, I can guess how she'd feel about taking on an infant nephew of her husband's that she hadn't known existed."

"But what about you, Nick?"

"No." He hadn't even paused for breath before giving the answer.

"Just...*no?*"

"Okay, you want the long version?" He looked angry, and there was another emotion in the mix that she couldn't pinpoint. "Here it is. I know nothing about babies or children."

"A lot of people don't when they become parents."

He ignored her. "I'm single. I'm fully involved in running an expanding corporation. The only thing I have to offer this child is financial support, and that, as I've said, I'm fully prepared to do. Sam will agree on that. The subject may not come up in this first visit today. I'd appreciate it if you'd keep my intentions confidential, Celie..."

"Of course."

"...because I need to check the facts of this woman's story first, and see what sort of a person she is. I want to see her, talk to her face-to-face, before any further decisions are made."

"I thought we were going to Cleveland to see the baby," Celie said.

She felt a painful disappointment at Nick's attitude, and realized how naive she'd been. Baby Carter was so real to her. She'd heard him in her dreams for weeks, and she'd worried the past two nights when he hadn't made a sound.

Sometimes she'd even seen him, the way she had

in that dream before the trip to New York a couple of weeks ago, but mostly he'd never quite been close enough. Mostly, she'd felt as if he were in the next room, and the dream had always faded too soon for her to get there in time. Knowing that she'd see him in another hour, and maybe even hold him in her arms, gave her an expectancy and a longing that she'd foolishly expected Nick to share.

But how could he?

He hadn't heard Carter crying the way she had.

Until two hours ago, he hadn't believed that Carter was real.

"Of course we're going to see the baby," Nick answered, the way he might have said of course they'd see the Statue of Liberty on a trip to New York. "But this is far more about getting a bead on Ellen Davis. I can't afford to have the corporation or Sam or my parents getting tangled in some stranger's crude attempt to trade on our success."

"Right. I understand. I guess."

He looked at her. "Don't get sentimental about this, Celie." His voice softened. "I appreciate your concern. And your interest. I even appreciate that you're getting sentimental. But don't."

Chapter Five

Nick and Celie reached Ellen Davis's suburban home at five-after-five.

She must have been waiting for them. Nick turned into the driveway, and before he'd even switched off the engine, the front door had opened and there she was. Comfortable figure, flyaway gray hair, huge smile on her face. Even to his doubting eye, her excitement was genuine.

She'd told him over the phone that she was a widow. Her husband had died about five years ago. They'd fostered babies and children all through their marriage, as well as having kids of their own. These days, she'd said, she only took on special cases.

Like Carter.

Nick and Celie climbed out of the car and walked up the stone path, between two modest stretches of manicured lawn. He went first, and held out his hand, but Mrs. Davis didn't even see it. Coming down the front steps to meet them, she reached her arms out, laughing and crying with pleasure and emotion, and she swamped Nick in an enormous hug before he could get out more than three syllables of a clipped, formal greeting.

He abandoned the attempt to speak and concentrated on dealing with the hug instead. He patted her back as he felt her chafing his, tried to bend a little lower because she wasn't very tall, and smelled fresh applesauce in her hair.

Carter's dinner.

Nick had seen baby food commercials on TV. He knew that mess happened with a baby.

"Is he awake?" he heard himself say, as if he'd totally forgotten that this woman could quite possibly be a cold-blooded scam artist, and his supposed half nephew no relation to him at all. He felt more than a little out of place in his expensive, hand-tailored charcoal business suit. It didn't fit in this setting.

"He's in his high chair," Mrs. Davis answered. "Come on in. Is this Mrs. Delaney?" She beamed at Celie.

"My executive assistant, Cecilia Rankin," Nick explained.

The woman didn't seem fazed. "Well, it's wonderful to meet you, dear."

She patted Celie on the arm, and Celie smiled at her and planted a kiss on her cheek. She immediately looked flustered about her impulse.

"I'm sorry," she said. "I somehow feel as if I know you, that's all." She frowned. "Uh...which is— Anyhow, we spoke briefly on the phone this afternoon, before I put you through to Nick."

Mrs. Davis led them back up the steps, which were bare of leaves and dust. Nick noted azalea bushes just about to bloom in their beds in front of the porch, and New Guinea impatiens with dark, glossy leaves, freshly planted in a neat pattern of alternating colors.

The inside of the house was similarly neat and well cared for, with hardwood floors and a hardwood staircase leading up to the left. Passing through a living area, and a room that could have been a dining room but was set up as a playroom, they reached a big country kitchen, and there sat the high chair with the baby strapped in it. He had applesauce all over his face and he was banging his little spoon on the plastic high-chair tray.

"Carter, here's your uncle Nick," Ellen Davis said. She spoke cheerfully and lovingly, but without the high-pitched, oversweet cooing sound that some women put on whenever they addressed a baby. She turned back to Nick. "Uncle Nick is what we should call you at this stage, right?"

"That seems appropriate," he managed to say, far more emotional than he'd expected to be.

Where was Celie? He flashed a glance over his shoulder and saw her hanging back in the doorway. She obviously thought this was his moment.

His and Carter's.

And maybe she was right.

He stepped closer. Carter dropped his spoon. He ignored it on the floor, and so did Nick. "Hi, little guy," he said.

The baby smiled. A big, wet, soft-lipped, beaming, toothless smile that danced in his brown eyes and flooded down into wildly waving little arms and made his whole body strain forward in the harness that held him safely in the chair. He let out a babbling sound.

"He's a handsome fellow," Nick commented.

It sounded so inadequate. It *was* inadequate, even though it was true. The baby had a silky fuzz of dark, golden-brown hair, cheeks like dimpled peaches, a button of a nose and those alert and lively brown eyes, set big and wide below a high forehead. He wore a stretchy sky-blue suit with a white duck embroidered on it, and he was a total cherub.

Nick struggled for something better than the "handsome" comment, and came out with, "Does he smile like this for everybody?"

"Right now, he does, as long as he's not tired and cranky. He's at that great age when his heart belongs to everybody. In six months or so, it'll be a different story. He'll have learned who he's supposed to be attached to."

"I guess so," he answered politely.

Was Mrs. Davis just making conversation, out of her vast experience of babies, or was it a more pointed comment. Who was Carter supposed to get attached to? Was she prodding him to consider the question?

"Some of 'em, when they're toddlers," she finished, "you can't even take a shower on your own without 'em crying for you."

"Good grief!"

"He's finished his meal, do you want to pick him up?"

Nick didn't even know which bits of a baby acted as handles, and this baby definitely looked breakable. Getting applesauce on his suit wouldn't be a big deal, but would the wool fabric be too rough on Carter's tender baby skin?

The apprehension must have showed in his face because Celie stepped up beside him.

"Could I?" she said.

He felt a rush of gratitude. Once again, Celie was here when he needed her. This wasn't exactly the kind of situation he'd hired her for, but that fact didn't seem important right now.

"Why, sure," Mrs. Davis answered. Deftly, she wiped the applesauce from the baby's face with a damp cloth and unclipped the harness. Carter kicked and wriggled as she lifted him out, then he grabbed a handful of her sleeve in his little fist.

She passed him across to Celie, and Nick saw his executive assistant's whole body change the moment the baby arrived in her arms. "Oh, he's just beautiful!" she said. "He's so right, and so perfect. I already feel as if I know him. I've been wanting to see him so much."

She smiled and tilted her head to look down at him. Nick realized that a baby didn't need to have handles. Carter just kind of locked into place on Celie's hip, with her hand on his diaper-padded bottom for support. Her other hand spread across the baby's back, but Carter didn't really need it there, so after a few seconds she took it away and touched her fingers to his cheek, still smiling the widest, softest smile Nick had ever seen.

Then her eyes filled with tears, and she had to clear her throat before she could speak.

"How much time did his mother have with him?" she asked Ellen.

"Nearly three months."

"So she got to see him smile?"

"She sure did. She was getting real sick by the end and was on a lot of medication, but when they're that little, they sleep a lot, so the two of them just cozied up to each other in bed. Doctors delivered him six weeks early. She wouldn't let them do it any sooner than that. But he was pretty healthy, right from the start, and the best behaved newborn you've ever met. As if he knew she needed him to be.''

Celie nodded. "That's something, then.''

Nick couldn't even speak.

"It was everything, for Jane," Ellen said. "That, and hoping to find the half brothers her mother had told her about. You had no idea about her, Nick?''

This time he was the one who had to clear his throat. "None. Seems like there should be some kind of memory. Visiting her in the hospital when she was born, or something.''

"Jane was sick when she was born. And when she wasn't in the hospital, she was with me. She didn't pick up until her three-month birthday. That was when your mother celebrated. Tried to, anyhow. She got a big ice-cream cake, all decorated with—''

"Dear Lord," Nick whispered. "An ice-cream cake? Then I do remember. That has to be where the memory is from.''

He'd told Celie about it, just a week and a half ago, and he could see it in his mind right now—that pretty, enticing picture of a pink ice-cream cake beginning to melt in the refrigerator. It wasn't just a memory, now. It was attached to a baby sister.

Celie looked at him with her big, beautiful eyes. She hadn't forgotten what he'd told her. "Here," she said. "It's your turn.''

And before he knew it, he had Carter in his arms and locked onto his hip, just the way Celie had held him. "Hi," he said. "Hi, little guy." He tried touching the baby's face the way she had, and he tried smiling at him. Carter beamed back, and started bouncing his little body.

"He had a big nap this afternoon," Ellen said. "Four hours. He's full of energy now. Want to take him out in the yard for a bit? There's a swing set, and he can handle the baby one, if you strap him in nice and tight and push him real gentle."

"Shall we, Nick?" Celie said. Her whole face was eager and bright.

This was already more than he'd intended.

Different to what he'd intended, certainly.

On the phone, Ellen had mentioned documentation—birth and death certificates, adoption records—and he'd imagined himself studying that with all the attentiveness he was now giving Carter instead. He hadn't been able to picture the baby in his mind at all, hadn't been prepared to find him anywhere near this cute.

The way he felt now, the documentation could wait.

"Okay," he said. "Yes, let's do that."

He transported the baby like a fragile piece of china, through a glass door that opened from the playroom onto a deck still bathed in late sunshine. Steps led down from the deck into the yard, and the swing set was fixed into the soil in front of two trees clothed in blossom. The trees had dropped a carpet of petals onto the grass, and it looked like pale pink snow.

He found it awkward to fasten Carter into the molded plastic seat of the swing, but Carter remained supremely tolerant of his clumsiness and smiled the whole time.

"Can I push him?" Celie said.

"Gently," Nick reminded her, as if he knew from

his own experience just how Carter liked to be pushed.

They took turns, and when the baby had finally gotten bored, Nick discovered that his whole face was tired from smiling.

Back in the house, Ellen had fixed food for them— coffee, a neat pile of sandwiches, some cookies and some cake. She'd also brought out the documentation he'd almost forgotten about. She put a baby-sized blanket on the floor, and propped Carter there with pillows in front of his baby gym. He batted away at the rattles and mirrors and whatnots, while the three adults sat at the table and ate.

Nick was hardly aware of Celie and Ellen chatting together as he studied the photocopied papers Ellen had given him. ''Our birth mother's name was Louise Taylor,'' he murmured. ''She doesn't list Jane's father on Jane's birth certificate, but she lists ours. Andrew Gray.''

He'd caught Ellen's attention. ''Common names,'' she said. ''Not real helpful in tracing more about your history.''

''I'm not interesting in doing that,'' he answered firmly, thinking of the loving parents who'd raised him since he was three. He wouldn't do anything that might hurt them or complicate their lives.

''Your mother never talked much about it, either,'' Ellen said. ''She died when Jane was fifteen, but by then they hadn't seen each other for a while.''

Nick studied the pages again. There was no suggestion that any of the documentation wasn't genuine, and nothing at all about this woman that raised alarm bells. Everything she'd told him was true, and Carter was the closest blood relative that he and Sam had in the world.

It was nearly six-thirty by the time they left. Ellen invited them to stay for a proper meal, but Nick turned her down, and she seemed to understand. "I need some time," he told her. "Just to process this."

"Of course you do."

"And I need to talk to Sam about what we want to do, what's best for everyone concerned, and also what's possible."

"There's no hurry." An almost imperceptible stiffness crept into her tone. Caution, maybe, rather than stiffness. Or even disappointment. Had she guessed that adoption wasn't on the cards? Was it too far-fetched to think she was that perceptive? She added, "It's a big decision."

"And there are several options," he reminded her. "Sam and I will be more than happy to cover any costs associated with Carter remaining in your care, including a full-time nanny to help you out. We also need to consider that there are thousands of couples in this country who are desperate to adopt, whereas that option doesn't fit Sam's or my situation right now."

She nodded. "This has come at you from left field," she said, as if all he had to do was take a few days to get used to the idea.

She was wrong.

Carter wasn't a puppy or a kitten. He was a lifetime commitment, and Nick was going to make a cool-headed, rational decision on his future, not act out of some touchy-feely sentiment that could vanish with a change in the weather.

"I'll be in touch very soon," he answered, his

voice deliberately clipped. "And if you get a chance to photocopy those documents for me in the meantime, that would be great."

For the return journey to Columbus, Nick insisted on taking the wheel and Celie didn't argue. The emotions of the afternoon had drained her, even more than the 150-odd miles she'd already driven.

For a while, she pretended to sleep, but felt wide-awake despite her fatigue. Opening her eyes, she watched Nick, who stared straight ahead, unaware of the way she was studying him. He'd flung his suit jacket onto the back seat, taken off his tie and rolled his pale gray shirtsleeves, but he didn't seem relaxed. His face looked as if it was carved from marble—impossible to read, unless marble gave off an emotion of its own.

Maybe it did. As she'd discovered on Tuesday night at the opening of the sculpture exhibition, marble was lovely to look at, and nice to have around. It was strong and reliable, also, but ultimately it was cold.

The idea that Nick might not adopt his nephew made her miserable. Too miserable. She didn't want to analyze too closely the complicated strands in the way she felt. This was her boss's life, she told herself.

His decision.

His past.

His baby.

Exactly. His baby. *His.*

He needed to want Carter. He needed to take the baby into his heart. She would be so disappointed, he would be so much less of a man, and she would never be able to forgive him, if he didn't do it.

But maybe he couldn't do it on his own. Maybe his troubled early years had left too much of a legacy.

Is this what the seamstress has been trying to tell me all along? Celie wondered.

The seamstress hadn't just wanted to tell her that the baby existed and needed to be found, but that Nick would need help fitting Carter into his life. It felt like a heavy responsibility for Celie to take on, especially at a point where, for her own emotional protection, she would much prefer to see less of her gorgeous boss, rather than more.

It's not up to me, she argued to herself. *It's up to Ellen and Sam and Nick's parents. Anyone but me. The decision is up to Nick most of all. How can I push him into something he doesn't want to do? It's not my role. I don't have that power.*

But what about Carter?

The seamstress would have said it, if she'd been here in the car. She wasn't, fortunately, so Celie could ignore her. Stubbornly, she snuggled lower in the front seat and pretended to doze.

She pretended so well that after about half an hour, as darkness fell, she really did doze and lost an accurate sense of time passing, until she felt the car slow and begin to make more frequent turns. Opening her eyes, she saw the gracious homes and wide lawns of Upper Arlington, and realized they'd almost reached Nick's house.

It had to be around nine. "Are you going to drop me home, Nick?" she asked, still fuzzy from sleep. Her silk top was badly creased.

"This is your car, remember," he answered. "And I'm not letting you go home, yet. Come in and we'll fix dinner. You need to wake up a bit, and get some food in your stomach.''

He pulled into his driveway and pressed the remote button for his garage door, which rose silently. It was a big garage, and her little compact fit easily inside beside his two vehicles.

Celie had never been to Nick's house before. She'd never needed to. It was a tribute to the new and more personal complexities in their relationship that she could find herself here, at nine o'clock on a Friday night, after a day that had brought out wildly swinging emotions in both of them.

She knew that Carter had touched his heart more than he wanted to admit, but she was also terribly afraid that it wouldn't be enough.

He ushered her through the connecting door from the garage to the house. They entered a carpeted hallway, with pristine, professionally designed wall treatments and decor. Celie knew Nick had bought this place about three years ago, when Delaney's had hit a new plateau of success. The house reflected his multimillionaire status.

She noted the plug-in points for a central vacuuming system, the control panel for an elaborate alarm, the huge rooms, the expensive furnishings, the original art on the walls. Following him, she eventually reached a kitchen that his Realtor would have described as ''restaurant quality.''

Looking around, she would have sworn that he'd never so much as opened a can in here, but she soon discovered she was wrong. He'd opened many things in three years, and he planned to open a few more tonight.

French champagne was first on the list. With the

bottle and two fluted glasses in his hand, Nick told Celie, "I want to celebrate Carter. And Jane. No matter how much Carter's existence might complicate my life and Sam's, it's something to celebrate and be happy about. You'll join me, won't you?" He untwisted the wire holding the cork in place.

"Yes, of course. I'm so glad you feel that way, Nick."

He gave her an enigmatic look, his thumbs easing the pressurized cork free.

She added defiantly, "Don't tell me I'm being sentimental."

He shrugged and smiled. There was a musical pop as the cork came out. "Okay." He placed it on the granite bench top.

Her heart flipped as she watched the crystal-clear liquid bubble into the glasses, giving off a smoky vapor. Nick had this all wrong. She was sure of it.

He gave her one glass, raised the other and said, "To Carter, and to Sam and me doing our best for him." He gave a complicated smile. End-of-the-day beard shadow had begun to darken the lower half of his face, and his blue eyes looked tired.

Celie sipped the dry, fragrant liquid. Its complex flavors tingled in her mouth, and she knew it had to be an expensive brand and an exceptional vintage. "Sam doesn't know about Carter yet," she realized aloud.

"I'm not going to hit him with this until he gets back from Mustique on Sunday."

"You're saying it would spoil his vacation?"

Nick was silent for a moment, then said reluctantly, "I don't want to say too much against my sister-in-law, but I think if Marisa heard about Carter, she'd spoil Sam's vacation for him, without any help from me. She won't want anything to do with a baby whose origins she's unsure of. She'll even argue against giving any financial support. If their marriage can be saved, I don't want to set the whole process back with a piece of disastrous timing.''

"That makes sense," Celie had to agree.

"Want to eat?"

"If I could see any food."

He opened the full-size freezer adjacent to the refrigerator. "My housekeeper freezes meals for me," he said. "*Huge* meals. I'm not sure if she wants me to have lots of company, or bulk me up to pro wrestler dimensions.''

Celie laughed. "Even with two of us, could we eat as much as a pro wrestler?"

"You'd be surprised. She's a fine cook. And she labels the containers like a restaurant menu so I know exactly what they are. Tonight, our choices are duck à l'orange with potato croquettes and seasonal vegetables, seafood in a herb, cream and white wine sauce on a bed of wild rice, or something that's just called pot-au-feu. I think her pen must have been running out on that one.''

"Okay, I'm groaning. How about we have all three? No, seriously, duck à l'orange sounds..." she held up her glass "...appropriate with the champagne.''

"Duck it is, then. All right, now what does she say?" he muttered to himself. "Microwave on medium for—"

"Are you sure this is a housekeeper? She sounds like an angel."

"I imagine she must be." He slid the lidded glass

dish into the microwave and pressed some buttons. "I got her through an agency, and I've only met her once. We maintain a warm and respectful written correspondence, however." He saw her expression. "You think that's weird, don't you? Cold, or something."

"You've never struck me as a cold person, Nick," she answered helplessly. Unconsciously, she leaned on the granite-topped island in the center of the kitchen and took a larger mouthful of the champagne than she'd intended, watching him. Sparkling flavor exploded in her mouth once again, and bubbled straight up to her brain. The microwave began to hum.

She struggled to work out the problem with Nick's attitude to his housekeeper, and realized that she'd somehow come to dislike the boundaries he put up between the different segments of his life. She hadn't disliked them before. She'd respected them, and shared them, but Carter had entered Nick's life now, and that changed everything.

"But you still think it's weird," he persisted.

"I think you have too many boundaries."

"Yet you like to maintain the appropriate boundaries yourself."

"I'm not sure what those are any more," she blurted out. "I'm not sure if boundaries like that should exist." She'd been thinking of Carter, but when her eyes met his, both of them were suddenly thinking of something else.

Tuesday night.

She hadn't maintained the appropriate boundaries then, and neither had he. She'd been the first one to come to her senses…or the first to lose sight of something very important. Which was it?

She didn't know anymore, and if Nick did, he wasn't acting on either possibility. He just kept standing there, slowly rolling the delicate stem of the champagne flute back and forth between his finger and thumb, watching her. The whole, huge, sparkling clean kitchen was filled with Celie's awareness of how much they wanted each other. It frightened her that they could communicate it so clearly without words and without taking a single step closer together.

Nick brought his champagne flute to his mouth, his eyes still fixed on her face. When he took the glass away again, his parted lips glistened with a film of liquid. Celie felt her breathing quicken. She tried to smile at him, as if this silence was casual and easy, but they both knew it was anything but, and she couldn't pretend.

"Do we need to set the table?" she finally asked, to break the tension.

"She leaves it set. With two places. Definitely seems like a hint, doesn't it?"

They both moved toward the swing door that led through to the large dining room, stopping in their tracks just before they got close enough to touch.

"Does *she* have a name?" Celie asked.

"Yes, she has a name." Nick took a step closer, and he looked impatient. "I even know it. Peg. And I buy her a gift at Christmas, without sending you to the mall to get it for me, Celie. So can we quit this?"

"Quit what?"

"The disapproval." He leaned his hand on the doorjamb at head height, which made him seem to tower over her. "The subtle suggestion that if I'm not best friends with my fifty-six-year-old housekeeper, then I'm not fit to make the right decision on how to incorporate Carter into my life. That's the subtext, here, isn't it?"

"I never—"

"I know you pretty well, Celie." He leaned closer, frowning at her, his eyes smoky. "I've gotten to know you even better just lately. I know what you think. But a few uncanny dreams don't give you the right to an input in my decision, or even an opinion on it."

"I'd have an opinion even without the dreams," she said.

"Well, keep it to yourself, in future."

"If that's what you want."

"And don't threaten to resign over it, because I need you."

"More than you know," she told him, thinking of what the woman in her dreams wanted her to do.

"Yeah, okay. More than I know," he answered. His gaze fell to her mouth. "More than I want to know."

He reached out and touched her face. If she'd pulled back at that point, maybe he wouldn't have kissed her. But she couldn't pull back, because desire had frozen her in place, and so he did. He kissed her. Again.

His lips were sticky and sweet from the champagne, and the taste of it mingled in their mouths as they explored each other. Celie tried not to touch him, because she was too afraid of what might happen if she did.

She held her hands out from her sides, closed her eyes and felt only his mouth on hers, warm and firm and utterly delicious. But she'd forgotten about the half inch of champagne still left in her glass and the glass tipped and spilled in her slack fingers, half onto her hand and half down to the floor.

Her exclamation told him what had happened. He reached for her hand and lifted it between them. He took the glass away and put it on the bench beside his, then raised her hand higher, to his mouth.

"Sticky," he said, and let the tip of his tongue run across her palm and along the sides of each finger, until it reached the sensitive web of skin where the fingers met her palm.

Celie went limp, giving him her hand as if she didn't need it anymore, and wanted him to have it forever. When the stickiness had gone, he laced his fingers through hers, dropped their hands to thigh level and twisted their two arms together, anchoring her in place so he could cover her mouth with his once more.

They kissed until the microwave switched off, with several very annoying beeps. The beeps stopped, and Nick muttered, "It can sit," and kept on kissing her. The flavor of orange-scented gravy seeped in their direction. The flavor of their kiss got stronger and better every second.

Celie shook her hand free of Nick's and ran it up his arm until it came to rest on his shoulder. It felt hard with muscle and she massaged it, stroked it, explored it, so she could find out more about how those muscles felt, and how they moved. Her knuckles brushed his neck, which felt warm and smooth, and had the most delicious curve in it, so she abandoned his shoulder and explored his neck, instead.

Then she discovered his hair, and the shape of his head.

Nick groaned as she combed her fingers upward, and his arms tightened around her, sliding against the silk of her top. Her breasts squashed against his chest and her nipples began to ache with pleasure.

Her hips rocked as if her whole body was a whip that someone had cracked in slow motion, and her breasts shimmied across Nick's shirtfront in the same rhythm. She liked everything about the way their bodies moved with each other, and pressed closer, winding her arms around his neck, rocking those hips in slow figure eights, letting him feel her hardened nipples and her ravenous mouth.

She never wanted this to stop.

Nick shuddered, and groaned again. "Do you feel what you've done to me?" he whispered.

"Yes," she whispered back. She parted her lips further, and stole another kiss. "I'm impressed with myself, to tell the truth." Although she hadn't intended to, she was confessing something important with these words. They didn't come out like a confession, however, they came out like an invitation—creamy and seductive.

"You're supposed to be impressed with me," Nick said, with a smile in his voice. "Aren't you?"

"I'm very impressed with you." She breathed the words into his mouth. "But that's nothing new, and nothing unexpected. The rest of it... Well, it is. A bit new, I mean."

"What are you saying, Celie?" He pulled his mouth away, put his hands on her shoulders and looked into her face. "You didn't know you could respond this strongly? You didn't know you could make me react the way I am?''

Her confidence faltered. "I— Not really. I mean, I knew. In my head. But it's never been like this before. I haven't had…uh…a lot of experience.''

"Why not?''

"Lots of reasons. Taking care of Mom, and watching a couple of my friends make some mistakes I didn't want to repeat. It hasn't been a big deal.'' Until now. "Hey, you're blowing the mood, Delaney,'' she accused him shakily.

"No, I'm not.'' He kissed her again, and murmured, "That's not the plan, anyhow.''

Apparently, the plan was to slip his hands inside her top and bring them higher until he reached her breasts. When he got there, cupping her through the lace of her bra, she gasped with the pleasure of it and let her throbbing nipples jut forward as her head stretched back.

Nick set a trail of kisses arrowing up her throat, and said, "If this is new, then we have to make it even better.''

"Mmm, is that possible?''

"Oh, yeah. It's possible.'' His tone changed suddenly. "It's possible,'' he repeated. His hands slowed on her body, then stopped. "But I wonder if it's really what we want. We talked about this the other night. *You* talked about it.''

"Today changed things,'' Celie said. "Today made everything harder. When I drove you to Cleveland. Seeing Carter.''

She didn't mention her dreams, but Nick didn't need her to. He must have understood the deeper meaning to what she'd said when she held the baby in her arms.

I feel as if I already know him.

And of course she'd known Nick for months, cared about him for months. Just how personal that care could get, she didn't yet know, but she did know that Ellen Davis's phone call this afternoon had raised the stakes hugely. If Nick hadn't had the power to hurt her before, he certainly had it now.

"I shouldn't have gotten you involved with the baby," he said. "I should have waited until I'd calmed down, or paged Leo."

Celie's scalp tightened. "What do you mean, you shouldn't have gotten me involved?" Her anger rose inside her, making her breathing stiff and painful.

"I should have left you out of it. There was no reason for you to see him."

"I was already involved, Nick, and I would have been even if I hadn't driven you to Cleveland. I've been involved ever since I first heard Carter crying in my dreams. Are you going to discount that and tell me again that it was a coincidence? I can't believe that anymore. Carter's crying, the message that came through to me about who he was, all of that was real."

"That part of it I can't explain, and don't particularly want to think about," Nick agreed, speaking slowly and cautiously. "But I said it just now, and I'll say it again. The dreams are uncanny, yes, but they don't give you any more right to have an input into a crucial decision in my life than Kyla would have into Sam and Marisa's marriage."

"I think you're wrong," Celie answered defiantly,

but inside she began to crumble at the forceful rejection he'd just delivered.

"You're important to me, and I don't want to lose you," Nick went on. "We've got this pretty powerful attraction to each other right now, also, which complicates things even further and which neither of us wants to take the risk of acting on."

"There, I agree."

In my sensible moments, she added inwardly.

Which seem to be evaporating rapidly.

"Maybe the attraction wouldn't have happened if we both hadn't been unusually emotional lately. So I'm going to say it, Celie. Butt out. If I need an input or an opinion from you about Carter, I'll ask."

She nodded, close to tears. "Pretty clear."

"And don't resign," he told her.

"You said that before."

"I wasn't sure if I'd gotten through. Shall we eat now?"

"You can eat. I'm going home." She turned in the direction of the garage.

"No, you're not."

"I'd rather go home."

"As your boss, I'm ordering you to stay and eat duck à l'orange with potato croquettes and seasonal vegetables, Cecilia Rankin. It's been a long day, and a long week. We'll sit at opposite ends of the table, if you want."

The table seated twelve. She controlled a sigh. "Opposite *sides* will do fine."

"Are you going to resign?"

"No."

"Good. Because I need you."

"You said that."

"Let me know when you want me to say it again."

The answer to that would be, *Never!* Celie thought, because every new way that he needed her made it harder for her to hold back on needing him.

Chapter Six

Celie closed the trunk of her sister Veronica's car, which was now loaded with their mother's two suitcases and her crutches, as well as enough of Lizzie's essential baby equipment to furnish half a baby store. Ronnie was taking Mom down to Kentucky, today, for a stay of several weeks, until the cast on her leg was ready to come off.

Celie had left Nick's last night after taking the minimum possible time to eat duck à l'orange, and he hadn't tried to stop her. He hadn't come close to kissing her again, and neither of them had mentioned Carter's name. While they were eating, they'd talked about the three new Delaney's restaurants in Southern California that were scheduled to open next week, as if it was the most important thing on both their minds.

In her apartment a little later, Celie had stood in the middle of the floor and said to the silent rooms, "I'm sorry."

She hadn't told the apartment what she was sorry

for, but probably it and its former occupant already knew.

She was sorry for doubting the dreams.

She was sorry for failing to bring Nick and Carter together, even if it wasn't her fault.

Sometime this weekend, she'd decided as she stood there, she would go back to her hairstylist and get rid of the high, tight knot once and for all. She didn't want to be that knot-haired person anymore. She could hardly be angry with Nick for not letting Carter into his life, if she wasn't prepared to let in something new, either.

Now, with her hair appointment scheduled later this morning, Celie hugged her mom and helped her into the front passenger seat, which Ronnie had already extended as far back as it would go.

"Look after yourself, Celie, honey," her mom said.

"You, too, Mom. Don't get too ambitious, okay? Don't try to help Alex with the yard work. Make Ronnie wait on you hand and foot. Now, where's my Lizzie to say bye-bye to?"

"Already smiling for you, Celie," Veronica said. She had Lizzie in her arms.

Celie reached for the baby and held her close. Lizzie smelled like baby shampoo and sweet milk, and she was blond-haired, blue-eyed and gorgeous. She was only a few weeks younger than Carter, Celie had calculated, but she'd been blessed with such different circumstances. Would Nick's nephew ever get to call anyone Mom or Dad?

"You are a lucky little girl, sweetheart," she whispered to the baby. "I hope you'll always know it."

"What is your auntie telling you, Busy Lizzie?"

Ronnie crooned, taking her daughter and strapping her in her infant seat.

"Nothing important," Celie answered.

Nothing important to Lizzie herself right now, anyhow. Carter might one day feel differently.

Ronnie climbed into the car and drove off down the street. Celie watched them go, then finished various tasks in her mother's house, locked up and went to her hair appointment. Later, back home, when she came out to the front gate of the old Victorian to check her mailbox, there was a woman standing on the sidewalk, beside a tiny pink-wrapped baby in a carriage.

Another baby.

Wasn't there a saying that things came in threes?

Lizzie, Carter and now this new little girl.

The mailbox hinge squeaked as Celie opened it, and she couldn't imagine why she'd felt so strongly impelled to come out, in the middle of doing her laundry, and look inside. It contained only bills and credit card offers. She made a face at the sheaf of unappealing envelopes, tucked a strand of her new, chin-length haircut behind her ear and looked up to find the stranger with the carriage and baby still standing there, looking up at the rambling old house.

She smiled at Celie, and Celie asked, "Can I help you?"

She got the feeling that the new mother definitely wasn't admiring the evocative Victorian architecture, the ancient climbing roses trained around the posts on the porch or the half-finished renovation on the top floor.

"I'm sorry if it looked as though I was snooping," the woman said. "My name is Anna, and I used to live here. Anna Jardine. This house was good to me. I kind of wanted to come by and show off my new baby girl.''

"To the house?'' Celie answered, smiling a little.

"To the house, yes.'' The woman named Anna colored and laughed. She was around Celie's age, with a pretty smile, a tall, lean body and red-gold hair. "It sounds crazy, right? But, you see, I had the turret room apartment on the second floor, and…''

She stopped and waited, as if she had an inkling as to what Celie might say next.

Celie said it, with a sense of inevitability falling around her like a heavy Victorian velvet cloak. "That's my apartment, too.''

Anna tilted her head a little. "I wondered if it could be. Have you…'' She paused again, then went on cautiously, frowning. "…met her, then?''

Celie pretended not to understand, just in case she was wrong. "Met—?''

"Maybe you haven't.'' Anna stepped back a little, not with her feet, but with her tone. "I'm talking about the woman who sits sewing, or stands in front of her mirror, trying on her clothes.''

Celie nodded slowly and silently, and didn't need to say a word.

Anna clapped her hands together. "So you have? I *knew* it!''

"I've been having some strange dreams,'' Celie said. "Very real. I haven't known whether to— Until recently, I haven't wanted to believe that they were— You probably know how it feels.''

"Oh, I do!'' Anna said. "There are the dreams, and then she leaves you little items on the windowsill when you wake up.''

"A hat pin." Saying the words felt like confessing some dark, secret sin. The sin of believing in magic. Except that once Celie had confessed it, it didn't feel like a sin at all. The last weight of doubt fell away. "A scrap of fabric."

"Or a silk flower."

Anna opened her purse and took out a furled shape of faded pink and green. It was a tiny rosebud. Celie touched it with the tip of her finger, the way Nick had touched the hat pin at the restaurant ten days ago.

"It's beautiful," she said. "And you're right. It has to be hers."

"I've kept it in my purse ever since she gave it to me," Anna said. "I call her the Dream Stitcher."

"I like that. It fits her, doesn't it? It fits what she does."

"She must have done a lot of sewing during her life, whoever she was. I always got the impression she'd spent a lot of very happy hours in that turret room."

"She's very wise. Mothers me a little," Celie confessed.

"You're not kidding! I ate so many nourishing meals when I lived there."

"She cooked for you?"

"No, but she…kind of told me to look after myself, because I hadn't been, before then. At all. I was riding for a fall before I moved into that apartment, and I owe her a lot. This baby, for one thing." She smiled down at her child, asleep in the carriage.

"She seems interested in babies," Celie murmured.

Anna laughed. "You're getting me curious, now. I wonder what she's been telling you!"

"Oh, I probably shouldn't. It's not my secret."

"No?"

"It's a message for someone else."

"It must be important."

"It is. But he's not ready to hear it yet." Her stomach sank as she added, "I'm not sure if he ever will be."

"That would be sad."

"Worse than sad."

"Hey, Dream Stitcher, look at us," Anna said to the turret room windows. "We're talking about you. And I've brought you my baby to show off. Isn't she adorable?"

The baby began to stir, fretting in her sleep, and her mother said, "Uh-oh. I'd better keep moving, get her back to the car. We've had such a nice walk, Maybelle and I. I'm parked all the way down on King Street. You can't just drive up and park out front when you're visiting a ghost!"

"Is she a ghost?"

"Okay, yes, that's too scary, isn't it? And she's not scary at all. We won't call her a ghost. She's just the Dream Stitcher, and I'm glad you've met her."

"I'm glad I met you, too. I didn't tell you before. I'm Cecilia Rankin. Just Celie, usually."

"I'll probably come past again, sometime. Can I drop in and say hi?"

"I'd like that. Stay for coffee. I might have more to tell you by then."

"Good luck with our Dream Stitcher's message."

"Thanks."

They smiled at each other, and Anna began to push her baby carriage along the sidewalk toward the corner of the street.

Celie collected her mail and went back inside, with

a lot to think about, and a sense that her trip out to the mailbox at exactly that moment might have been part of the Dream Stitcher's plan all along. The idea didn't frighten her nearly as much as it would have done a week ago, and she felt a new certainty that the woman in front of the mirror had given her dreams about Nick's baby to the right person, after all.

Nick waited until Sam arrived at Delaney's corporate headquarters on Monday morning before giving him the news about their half sister and her baby.

He had Celie pick up a box of Sam's favorite chocolate-frosted doughnuts, made coffee for both of them and hauled Sam along to the conference room, where he shut the door and shut out the rest of the world. He'd already told both Celie and Kyla that they weren't to put through any calls.

"How was Mustique?" he asked his younger brother, as an ice-breaker. He handed over the hot mug of black coffee and opened the doughnuts.

Sam took one, looked at it blindly, then put it back. It wasn't a good sign.

"She loved it," he said. "She wants to live there. As well as in Paris and London and Rome and New York. Hell, Nick!" His voice shook. "Was she deliberately putting on a performance the whole time we were dating? All that stuff she said to me about not caring for money or fame or status, as long as we were together. I'm her meal ticket. Her à la carte, five-star, gourmet meal ticket, and she couldn't even be bothered to hide it anymore. She's so heartachingly beautiful, did I just not see the rest before?"

"You wouldn't be the first, bro," Nick answered.

"We're splitting up. It's hopeless. She checked into

a hotel last night, as soon as we got back. The crazy thing is, I can see exactly who she really is, now, but it doesn't stop my guts from burning over this. Love isn't a faucet you can just close off, it turns out, even when you want to. I'm going to have to talk to a good lawyer as soon as possible, because Marisa certainly will be. If this affects my input in the corporation over the next few months, then I'm sorry. I'll make it up to you when everything settles down, I promise.''

''There's nothing to make up,'' Nick said. ''Mom and Dad taught us that. It'll balance out. And even if it doesn't, we're brothers, so who cares.'' He put his hand on Sam's shoulder and gave it a squeeze.

''Yeah. Thanks.'' Sam stared into the coffee he hadn't yet touched.

He had darker coloring than Nick, and with his somber mood it gave him a brooding look, right now, that Nick didn't like. This wasn't the best day to have to break some major news, but he couldn't keep it from Sam any longer.

''Got a phone call on Friday,'' he said.

''Yeah?''

Nick took a deep breath before he launched into the story.

He and Sam didn't emerge from the conference room for another hour, and when they did the situation was pretty much as Nick had expected it to be. Sam had agreed that they should provide all the financial support that Ellen Davis needed, and that they should call their parents in Florida today to give them the news.

Meanwhile Sam had a divorce to organize.

Leaving him to find the right lawyer, Nick headed back to his office. He dropped by Celie's big, tidy desk on the way. She was tapping figures into her computer, but she looked up when she heard him come in. She knew why he'd been shut in the conference room with Sam for so long, and she wanted to know what Sam had said. Kyla had gone to the photocopy room, so it was safe to speak, and in any case, Kyla would have to be told the news soon.

"You'll be pleased to hear that Sam and I agreed," Nick told Celie on a drawl, well aware that she probably wouldn't be pleased at all.

They were due to fly to California together tomorrow, for two nights, and he didn't feel very confident about how the trip would go. On the one hand, they had a lot to get through. On the other, they would be in each other's company for ninety percent of their waking hours and all the activity in the world couldn't disguise the fact that they were tense with each other.

"Yes? You did?" Celie said. The eager response to his words surprised Nick at first. "He convinced you?" She went on. "Oh, that's great!" She stood up. "That's wonderful, Nick!" She looked so happy and bright-eyed that he realized his sarcastic phrasing had misled her completely.

"No, I just meant Sam agrees with me," he said quickly. "That we should support Carter, and have an involvement in his life, but leave him where he's best off. With Ellen. I didn't mean he agreed we should adopt."

"Oh. Of course." Her face fell, then she added in a bitter tone, "Silly me."

The delivery wasn't softened by the new haircut that swung around her face, nor by the pretty, feminine top and skirt she wore, teamed with dangly earrings and a matching gold necklace. She folded her arms across her chest and hunched her shoulders, as if she'd suddenly felt a chill.

"Sam and Marisa are getting a divorce," he told her angrily. Sam himself had stressed to Nick that he wasn't in any position to get involved in Carter's life right now.

"Oh," Celie said again. Her tone was even flatter this time. "Well, I guess we kind of saw that coming."

"We both agreed that we couldn't make a decision to adopt him lightly. The baby deserves better."

"Better than his own uncles?"

"Delaney's is opening twelve new restaurants this year," he reminded her. "How would Sam handle a baby, Celie? His head's a hundred miles away, right now, and he's in emotional hell. And how would I? Would I turn Carter over to a nanny for eighty hours a week, or more? How would that be doing the right thing by him?"

"He's flesh and blood. Don't you have to put that first? Just make it work, whatever it takes?"

Her eyes held both anger and appeal, and her cheeks had flushed that warm, gorgeous pink he'd never even known about until recently—until they'd started getting emotional with each other. He'd dreamed about Celie in various high states of emotion most of Friday night, and if the dreams she had were anywhere near as vivid, maybe he ought to believe in them more.

"The people I call mom and dad aren't flesh and blood," he said, fighting to hold on to what he believed. "By your logic, that makes them count less in my life. But they don't."

"That's true." She frowned. "I'm sorry, Nick. I didn't mean to belittle that relationship."

"Isn't it about finding what's best for Carter—the best parenting for him—not about biological ties?"

"Do you really believe you'd be a bad parent, then?"

"At the wrong point in my life, out of the blue, yes!" he told her, and he meant it.

"Okay, and how's Carter going to feel, one day, when he discovers that his time of need, his whole *existence,* didn't happen at some mythical, convenient 'right time' in your life? Why is this the 'wrong point,' Nick? Isn't that a question that you need to consider?"

"I don't know!" he almost yelled. "Do I? Does it matter why? And is it any of your business?"

"No," she answered. "I guess it's not."

He saw the way her angry confidence suddenly faltered, but turned and headed for his office anyhow, without another word, and without looking back.

The trip to California began badly. Mechanical problems with their flight delayed it by over an hour, during which Celie, Nick and the other passengers sat in their seats, waiting to be updated on the status of the problem. In Los Angeles, they were stalled on a freeway within ten minutes of leaving the airport. The air was hot and brown with smog.

Their delayed meetings ran late, and it was eight o'clock in the evening—eleven o'clock, Ohio time— when they finally checked into their hotel. Celie just wanted to hide in her room and eat comfort food in bed. Last night, she'd given herself permission to do exactly that, and she'd slept like a log until the alarm had sounded at six.

No dreams.

The Dream Stitcher didn't have anything new to tell her, Celie guessed.

She missed the dreams, but could still feel the welcoming personality that seemed to seep out of the apartment itself. She hadn't found any heating valves mysteriously switched off since Friday night, nor any other signs that her behavior had earned the disapproval of her ethereal roommate. Instead, her chandelier had gleamed more brightly, her antique clock had ticked with a more resonant music, and her hot water never seemed to run out.

Unfortunately, she knew she couldn't cocoon herself in the same way tonight. She and Nick had work to prepare for tomorrow, which would be a late, tiring day as well, because they had the opening of Los Angeles' first flagship Delaney's tomorrow night.

Nick called from his suite, one floor above, just as she finished hanging her outfit for tomorrow in the closet. "Want to come up here and we'll grab room service?" he said. "I went down and checked out the restaurant, but it looked full and there was a line. There's a conference on."

"Room service sounds great."

"Check out the menu, tell me what you want and I'll order it from here. Come up when you're ready. We'll get through the work stuff as quick as we can."

She ordered pasta and salad, and Nick called her back again a little later. "They said forty minutes, so there's no hurry. I can't think through tomorrow on an empty stomach."

The bath beckoned, and so did the sachets of

scented bath crystals arranged beside the porcelain sink. Celie took a long soak. She would have put on her robe afterward, except that she had a public elevator to go up in, with her boss waiting for her at the end of the journey. She hated having to dress again, but at least her muscles felt relaxed and loose, and the nagging headache behind her eyes had faded.

When she arrived in Nick's suite, the room service waiter had only just left, having laid everything out on the table as perfectly as Nick's invisible housekeeper, Peg, might have done.

He looked as tired as she felt, with jacket and tie removed and shirt unbuttoned several inches. "I'd rather prepare for tomorrow's meetings over breakfast instead, if that's okay with you," he told her.

"That's fine. Better," she agreed. "I couldn't concentrate anymore."

After this, they ate in silence, until he said, "You smell like you had a bath. Was it good?"

"Great. Recommended. I turned the spa jets on." She smiled, self-conscious. "But if you can smell my skin from the far side of the table, then I used too many gardenia bath crystals."

"That's the scent?" He smiled back. "Gardenia?"

He inhaled, leaning forward a little, as if his nose was pressed to her skin—the nape of her neck, maybe, or the valley between her breasts—and suddenly it didn't matter that she'd put on her travel-worn skirt and silk knit top after the tub, instead of the hotel bathrobe.

This was still too dangerous.

Her body began to tingle, and she remembered every detail of the way she'd felt in his arms on Friday night, and every bit of evidence that he'd been just as overwhelmed by the chemistry between them. Through the open door that led from the suite's sitting room to the bedroom, she glimpsed a king-sized bed, its covers already turned down by a maid, and mint chocolates sitting on each pillow.

A picture flashed into her mind, like an image from a movie. Tangled sheets. Naked skin. Entwined limbs.

That bed was so close. This hotel suite was so anonymous, and so private. If he touched her, if he kissed her, she didn't know where she'd find the strength of will to resist.

"I'll go as soon as I'm done here," she gabbed. "I'm wiped. It must be almost one in the morning by now, Ohio time."

"Just on," he agreed, glancing at his Swiss watch. "Don't hurry to finish, Celie. It's okay."

"I'm fine. I'm not very hungry this late." She ate one more token mouthful then stood up, still brushing a crumb from her lips with a napkin.

Nick didn't argue anymore. Instead, he accompanied her to the door and opened it for her. Aware of him so close behind her, Celie was ready to slip through it at once, with a short, polite phrase about seeing him tomorrow.

When would this stop happening? When would she be able to feel his body in her personal space without it pulling on her, without his masculine scent filling her nostrils and sending her dizzy with need?

"See you in the—" she began, but he cut her off with a hand on her arm.

"I didn't tell you before," he said. "Ellen Davis called while I was waiting for our meal. I'd tried to reach her before our flight departed this morning, and I'd left the hotel phone number on her machine."

She turned. "Carter's all right, isn't he?"

"Yes, he's fine." Nick leaned his arm on the open door. The suite's entry light wasn't switched on, and this section of the room was dim, making his eyes seem darker as Celie looked at him. "He was fast asleep, of course. I just wanted to touch base with her, when I called this morning. She says he's really starting to sit up well now, even better than he was last week."

"Why are you telling me this, Nick?"

Why are we standing so close, she added in her head, *when I was so determined it wouldn't happen?*

"I meant to tell you while we ate," he said. "I thought you'd be interested."

"In Carter's progress, or in the fact that you called Ellen?"

He shrugged, making his white shirt pull tight across the shoulders. "Both. Is that okay?"

"You told me on Friday night you regretted getting me involved."

He studied her face and sighed. "And that's true. But I guess I'm not happy that you think I'm handling this so wrong, Celie. We approve of each other at work. In a personal context, apparently we can't."

"That's a good argument for keeping things separate, I guess," she murmured, although she was pretty sure she didn't believe in such boundaries anymore.

"I wanted to show you that I'm interested in him, and I care about what happens to him. I really want you to see that. I just can't have him in my life, that's all."

Inwardly, Celie debated letting the issue go. She could easily tell herself it was Nick's life, and none of her business. But the dreams of Carter crying that had filled her nights had made it her business, some-how. Anna Jardine's Dream Stitcher *wanted* it to be her business, and she couldn't maintain a professional distance over this.

"Maybe it would be better for both of you—you and Carter, yes, and Sam, too—if you hadn't been given a choice," she said bluntly. "If there'd been no one else in the picture who could have taken care of him."

Nick swore, and knots of tightened muscle appeared on either side of his jaw. "You still think I'm taking the easy way out, don't you?" His teeth gritted together.

"I think Ellen Davis is spoiling you a little bit, yes," she said.

"Well, think again. One of her former foster children has a baby due. It'll be a scheduled cesarean just over a week from now in Chicago, and Ellen asked me tonight if I'd take care of Carter for the weekend so she could go up there and help out when the new mom comes home from the hospital."

"What did you tell her?"

He gave a short laugh. "I told her I'd do it, of course. Did you really think I'd turn her down? I'm aware of what she's trying to do, but that doesn't mean I have to fall for it. I'll look after Carter as best I can, and deliver him back when the weekend's over."

Celie asked, "Are you nervous?"

She thought about her niece, and how she would feel if her sister asked her to take care of Lizzie for a whole weekend on her own—changing diapers, folding and unfolding the elaborate stroller that Ronnie and Alex had bought, waking in the night to get bottles of milk and warm them just right—with no one to consult or share the load with.

Ronnie said she could tell just from the way Lizzie cried whether she was hungry or tired or bored or in pain. Celie wondered how quickly you could develop a skill like that. She'd adore to look after her niece for a weekend, but all the same she'd be—

"Terrified," Nick said. "But I'm going to hire a nanny to help."

"Right," she nodded. Thinking of Lizzie again, it didn't sound like such a bad plan. "From an agency?"

"I'll call one as soon as we get back."

"I can make a list for you, if you want."

"No, I'll handle it." For a few seconds, he looked at her without speaking, then said, "Okay, I'm waiting, Celie. Where's the condemnation?" There was a nuance of danger in the way he drawled the words. He leaned toward her, with a challenging glint in his eye and she lifted her chin, while deep inside her the familiar awareness coiled.

"I'm not condemning the idea," she said. "I'm really not, Nick. It's probably the best thing to do."

Nick almost looked disappointed, as if he'd wanted a battle. "She's driving down next Friday afternoon with him and his gear," he said. "And taking a flight from Columbus to Chicago."

"When's she picking him up?"

"Around noon on Monday."

"Three nights."

He grinned. "Yes, I can count." He added softly, "Now, will you do as I've asked before and butt out?"

She didn't answer him directly. She didn't want to

make a promise she might not be able to keep. Instead, she just slipped past him through the open door and said, over her shoulder, "Good night, Nick. I'll see you in the morning."

Chapter Seven

"Hello, Mr. Delaney!" Standing at Nick's front door, the weekend nanny from the agency smiled brightly, then brought a tissue to her face and kept it there for several seconds. The young, dark-haired woman had red, weepy eyes and a matching nose. She really didn't look well.

"What's wrong?" he asked bluntly. "Are you sick?"

"It's just a cold, I think," she answered, her tone far too perky. "I'm sure I'll be fine when I've taken something for it." She smiled again, trying to reassure him. Either she didn't want to let him down, or, since she was a part-time college student, she needed the work.

Nick wasn't happy. She didn't look like she'd be fine anytime soon.

Ellen would be here with Carter within the next half hour. How would they both feel if the baby got sick in his care? And he didn't like the idea of the nanny popping cold medication, either. Some of those products could really knock you out. The label might only warn against operating heavy machinery, but a baby was every bit as complicated, and a lot more fragile and precious.

Great! he thought. Just great!

It wasn't Ms. Palmer's fault that she'd gotten sick, and the agency might be able to send a replacement at short notice, but he'd taken the trouble to interview her, explain a little about Carter's history and show her over the house on Tuesday, and he'd checked out her references personally. He didn't want to grab a last-minute substitute, who couldn't possibly get here until after Ellen had left. He didn't want Carter's foster mother to have any doubts about the way he was handling this.

"Come in for a minute," he told the nanny. "I'm going to send you home, because you're not well, but I'll write you a check for your time."

Ms. Palmer was polite enough not to look at the check until after she left, but Nick knew he'd been generous. Neither she nor the agency could possibly complain.

His own problem remained unsolved, however.

The obvious solution occurred to him pretty fast.

Celie.

After all, half the purpose of her professional existence was to keep things running smoothly for him, to solve problems, to help him out of difficult situations.

Yes, but this wasn't her professional existence under discussion right now. This was personal—a part of his life that hadn't existed a few weeks ago, and that he wouldn't have imagined he'd ever let her in on, even if he'd known about it. Just last week, he'd asked her to butt out.

Cursing under his breath, Nick went to his study and found the number of the nanny agency on the notepad he kept beside the phone. He picked up the receiver, keyed in the digits, then cut the connection before it could start to ring. The next phone number he didn't need to look up. It was right there on his speed dial.

"Hi, Celie," he said into the phone a few seconds later.

"You want *me?*"

"Someone I can trust. Someone I don't have to explain anything to. Someone who knows at least a little bit about babies. You were so good with Carter two weeks ago."

"One hug. A play on the swing. I'd love to help," she told him, "but I'm…" She trailed off.

He helped her out. "You're surprised? After I told you to butt out?"

"That," she agreed. "I'm also not going to claim to be an expert."

"If you want me to apologize for the butt-out thing, then I will."

"I'll forgive you for the butt-out thing if you'll understand that I've only changed Lizzie's diaper twice and I wouldn't have won any awards for my technique."

"That's twice more diapers than I've changed in my life. How soon can you get here?"

"How much more do you want me to get done in the office?"

It was only three on Friday afternoon, and he'd left

her with a list. He didn't care about the list anymore. "Forget the office. Just get home, pack your overnight bag and come on over."

"You want me to stay over?" She sounded a little horrified. He might have been horrified, also, if he hadn't been even more horrified by the imagined picture of himself at three in the morning with a wide-awake, upset little nephew whose needs he didn't even begin to understand.

"Isn't that when babies are at their worst?" he said. "In the middle of the night?"

"I'll be there in an hour," she answered. Her voice gave nothing away.

Ellen arrived with Carter fifteen minutes later. It took several minutes just to unload the car. There was the car seat, a huge baby change bag, a portable crib, a packet of diapers and an overnight bag containing more changes of outfits than a supermodel would need for a three-week vacation.

"In case you don't get a chance to do laundry," Ellen explained.

Carter himself stayed asleep in the car seat when she carried it carefully into the house, and Nick made a mental note of the soothing, almost stealthy walk she used. He'd have to learn how to do that. Obviously once you'd gotten a baby to sleep, you wanted him to stay that way as long as possible.

The little guy certainly looked adorable, tucked into his seat with a light cream blanket over him. His cheeks were rosy, and his lashes as thick and dark and soft as an artist's sable paintbrush.

"The nanny got sick and couldn't make it," Nick told Ellen. "But I have a...uh...friend coming to help out, so don't worry."

Darn it, why was he talking this way? He was co-owner of a large and highly successful corporation. He didn't need to sound so apologetic, so approval-hungry, so uncertain.

Ellen didn't look as if she was worried.

"You'll be fine," she said. "He's not a difficult baby, compared with some I've cared for. Compared with my own four, either, come to think of it."

"Well, that's good to know," he answered feebly.

He knew by now that Ellen had kids, foster kids, grandkids and foster grandkids scattered across half the country. If there was a Fortune 500 list of expert moms, she'd be on it, right near the top. She found caring for babies as easy as he found reading a financial spreadsheet. He firmed his expression so that she wouldn't guess how spooked he was about this.

"Do you want to stop in for coffee?" he asked.

"I should get to the airport. I'd hate to miss the flight."

She gave him one of her big, warm hugs, and two or three final instructions that immediately meta-morphosed into garbled nonsense in his mind, and drove away a few minutes later, not scheduled to return for another sixty-nine hours.

Not that Nick was counting, or anything.

He wandered into his big, masculine living room, with its state-of-the-art sound and video systems, its slate-blue leather couches and its original oil paint-ings, where Ellen had put Carter in the middle of the Persian rug. At first he appeared peacefully asleep, but as Nick watched, he stirred and stretched and made some sucking sounds. Nick held his breath, then the baby settled again. He looked at his watch.

Celie should be here in around twenty-five minutes. Not that he was counting, or anything.

Nick looked relaxed and confident when he opened his front door to Celie at just on four o'clock. In contrast to her dressier work clothes of skirt, top and heels, he wore jeans, white cross-trainers and a thin knit cotton sweater in navy blue, with the sleeves pushed up to the elbows. He had a mug of steaming coffee in his hand.

"Want some?" he asked, when he saw her glance fall on it.

"That'd be good, thanks."

She'd seen him drinking coffee many times before, but in eight months of working together she'd never seen him this casually dressed. He always looked impressive in his expensive suits, even when he let go a little and took off the jacket and tie, but he didn't look like this—so fit and physical. The jeans and the sweater both conformed to his body in loving detail, showing plenty of muscle and not a skerrick of fat.

He must work out, and regularly. Celie had never seen him do it, never heard him refer to it, but he had to, with a body like that. She decided, fast, that she preferred to see him in his suits. They were less… less… They were more Nick Delaney the corporate employer, and a lot less Nick Delaney the man.

She was glad she hadn't changed between the office and here. Her heeled shoes and work skirt just might remind her of the boundaries she still needed to keep in place.

Meanwhile, she registered, there was no sign of Carter. Nick put his finger to his lips and said, "Still asleep in his car seat in the living room. He arrived here that way." This might explain the confidence and relaxation the man exuded more than he himself would have been willing to admit.

"Is there a spare room where I can put my bag?" Celie asked.

"Upstairs. Come on, I'll show you."

Nick definitely worked out. Following him up the stairs, to the upper level where she'd never been, she had his tight, masculine rear end right in her line of sight and was forced to appreciate the neat triangle it made with the wide reach of his shoulders.

Two doors to the right, when they'd gotten to the top of the stairs, she had her answer to the question about working out. He had his own personal gym. She glimpsed an array of impressive equipment, and saw on his sit-up bench the hollowed shape where his head must rest when he used it. The equipment wasn't just there for show.

The room across the corridor from the private gym turned out to be hers for the weekend. With its own adjoining bathroom, containing a tropical aquarium built into the wall, it was furnished as if his parents were the most frequent visitors. The queen-sized bed was covered in a gorgeous wedding-ring pattern quilt that looked handmade, and there were several high-quality pieces of antique furniture, including a tall-boy, a dresser and a bookshelf filled with a mixed assortment of reading material.

"Make yourself at home," Nick said. "And come down for that coffee when you're ready. If Carter gives us a quiet night tonight, I might feel like an expert, this time tomorrow, and let you go home."

Carter chose this moment to announce that he was awake.

Make that awake *and* upset.

"Oh," Nick said. "Okay. I guess it couldn't last forever. I guess they cry when they wake up." He headed for the stairs.

"I'll come with you," Celie offered.

She followed him down to the baby, but never got as far as the coffee Nick had promised.

Carter didn't stop crying.

Discussing the problem in depth, both adults first concluded that he must have had a bad dream, but when all their smiles and coos and distractions couldn't make him happy after several minutes, they began to wonder about his foot going to sleep, or his diaper getting uncomfortable, or a thread from his little blue suit wrapping itself tight around his toe. Celie knew this had happened to Lizzie once.

Nick rubbed the baby's feet and checked for loose threads, but didn't find any. Celie changed the diaper, aware that her boss was standing right beside her, taking mental notes on how it was done. Or, at one point, how it *wasn't* done. Celie almost put the new diaper on back to front. Carter had lovely smooth skin on his bottom, with no sign of a rash, so that couldn't be the problem.

"I guess some babies get rashes, don't they?" Nick said, frowning down at his little nephew, kicking and crying on the couch where Celie was working over him. "You put zinc cream on it, right?" He'd apparently learned a few useful things from TV commercials. "What if he gets one this weekend? I don't want to hand him back to Ellen with a problem he didn't have when she left."

"Let's not borrow trouble," Celie suggested.

She straightened and picked Carter up. His cheeks were red from crying, and he sounded louder than she'd have thought possible, given his size. Nick stepped closer and peered at him with a worried face. He patted Carter's back and his head, his own shoulder nudging Celie's without him appearing to notice.

To a stranger's eye, they would have made a very neat-fitting little unit—two inexperienced parents and their firstborn child, but Celie tried her best not to think about that.

"Let's see if we can cheer him up, before we think about rashes," she said. "Did Ellen say when he'd need a feed? Could it be dinner or bottle time for him?"

"She said a couple of things, just as she left. I...uh...didn't take all of it in," Nick confessed. He began to pace, like a lion in its cage. "But, yes, let's try a bottle. It couldn't hurt, right?"

They found the bottles and the can of formula in Carter's baby change bag, along with his little jars of pureed apricot and carrot and apple, and took everything into the kitchen. The instructions on the can were easy to follow, and Carter sucked happily, as if they'd gotten it just right.

Celie settled him deeper into the crook of her elbow and sat down in one of the two chairs at the round, café-style table in the corner of the big room. She loved how warm he felt, and how ardently he sucked, as if the whole of his body was involved.

"There!" Nick said, when the only sound in the kitchen came from the whistlelike sing of bubbles forming in the bottle. "He was hungry. That wasn't so hard."

But it didn't last. Carter finished the bottle and they spread out a baby blanket on the Persian rug in the living room for him to play on. He lay there on his tummy for a minute or two, then started to cry again.

"Maybe he wants to be on his back," Nick suggested.

They tried it, but Carter rolled right back on his tummy, crying the whole time.

"Maybe he wants a toy."

Apparently not.

"Maybe he just wants to be held."

Celie stood up from her anxious, perched position on the edge of the couch, but Nick got there first. He swooped down, gathered the baby in his arms and began to bounce him gently against his shoulder, as if he'd forgotten he'd never done this before. Celie was impressed. Such a big man, acting so gentle. But Carter didn't stop crying.

"Fretting," she said. "It's more like fretting, isn't it?"

"Did he have enough to drink?"

"A whole bottle. He couldn't be tired, after sleeping the whole way from Cleveland in the car."

"Maybe he could. Shall I set up the portable crib and see if we can settle him back to sleep?"

"He only has a portable crib?"

"Isn't that okay?" Nick looked concerned.

"My sister says she finds it hard to soothe Lizzie to sleep in hers because it's so low, its awkward to bend down to."

"I bought a change table and a high chair, I didn't buy a crib."

"No, I guess you didn't. Let's set up the portable crib. Where's it going?"

"In my room."

His room. He planned to put Carter in his own room.

Celie hadn't expected that.

The little kick of disappointment that she had felt because Nick hadn't thought it worthwhile to buy a crib went away. In its place came a flood of mixed feelings that she couldn't identify at first. Happiness, yes, and hope, but something else, too.

It couldn't be loneliness, could it?

She couldn't possibly be feeling *left out,* as if the fragile new bond Nick had begun to build with his nephew was hurtful to her because she wasn't included. That would be crazy, and wrong. She wanted Nick and Carter to bond, the stronger the better. And of course she couldn't be included in that bond. She wouldn't even be here if his nanny hadn't gotten sick.

"Can you take him?" Nick said. "And I'll carry the crib upstairs."

Celie patted and bounced Carter, the way Nick had done, to try to settle him, but without much success. If she really worked at it, she could coax him to quieten and smile, but as soon as she cut the circus clown stuff, his little face would screw up again and he'd start to fuss, his fist grabbing at her sleeve.

Nick's bedroom was enormous, with space for three king-sized beds instead of just the one he actually had. There was plenty of room for the crib. He wrestled with it for a minute or two, cursing the instructions and acting like a rodeo cowboy breaking a new horse. He soon got it to rattle and spring into shape, however, and found the quilts and scallop-edged white and blue flannel baby sheets Ellen had packed.

"Okay, now do we just put him in it and tell him

it's night-night time?'' he said, but not as if he really expected Celie to have an answer.

She tried her best. ''Well, I know my sister puts Lizzie on a breast and she gets all drowsy and transfers to her crib with no problem.''

''Carter doesn't look drowsy, and we don't have a breast.'' He looked at Celie. At her face, and then a little lower down. ''Okay, we do have a breast, in fact two, and they're very— But they don't—'' He stopped. ''You know what I mean.''

''I know what you mean.'' She laughed, flushed and began to heat up, while Carter tried to bury his face in her shoulder. ''Let's put him in, and sing a lullaby, and close the drapes, and tiptoe out of the room.''

''Sounds good. I'll handle the drapes, you take the lullaby.''

The room darkened, and Celie began to sing. '''Hush little baby, don't say a word...''' She laid Carter down on his back and brought the sheet and quilt up to his chin, singing softly with each action. He kicked the covers off immediately, and kept crying. '''If that diamond ring turns to brass,''' Celie sang.

She covered Carter.

He kicked the covers off.

''Maybe he's warm enough without them,'' Nick suggested.

'''Mama's gonna buy you a looking glass,''' Celie sang, nodding.

''I'll just...'' Nick tiptoed toward the door, then waited there, watching.

Celie kept singing. Carter cried louder. She got to the end of the song, and Nick held the door open for her. He followed her out of the room and closed the door behind him, and Carter cried. The sound seemed to penetrate the door as easily as a nuclear warhead would have done.

Standing close, Nick and Celie looked at each other, shoulders and mouths drooped, suffering.

"Can you do this?" Nick said, his voice strained and hoarse. He put his hand on her arm. "Can you go downstairs and leave him, while he's like this?"

"No."

"Neither can I."

"Do you have Ellen's number in Chicago?" Celie asked.

"She wouldn't be there yet. She'd still be in transit. Anyhow, do I want to admit, after two hours, that Carter is totally rejecting our baby-care strategies?" He looked at his watch. "Make that two and a half hours."

"Six-thirty? Already?"

"Let's go pick him up again." Nick burst through the door, bent low over the crib and lifted Carter as if his crying was the ticking of a time bomb, due to go off in another millisecond.

"Hey, kid," he said, in a soothing, tender voice that Celie had never heard him use before. He swayed back and forth from foot to foot, slowly and rhythmically as he spoke. "I have to tell you, your signals are about as clear as computer error messages. Yeah, I know you're not happy. I'm perceptive. I get that part. But could you give us more of a clue about why? Is it the state of the Amazon rainforest? Is it the economy? Are you just missing Ellen?"

"You're good at that, Nick," Celie couldn't help saying.

"Yeah, but it's not helping, is it?" Carter rubbed the side of his little head against Nick's face, and Nick's tone changed. "Hey, does he feel warm to you?"

"He felt fine when I put him in the crib. I don't think he needed the covers."

"No, I mean fever warm. Hot. Like he's getting sick."

"Sick?" Celie stepped closer and laid the palm of her hand on Carter's forehead. It did feel warm. Not sleepy baby warm, as she'd unconsciously assumed before, but fever warm, as Nick had said. "Do you have a thermometer?"

"No. I never get sick. And when I do, I know it, without taking measurements."

"Ellen could have packed one in his bag."

They looked, but couldn't find one, and Nick decided aloud, "Anyhow, what would that tell us? He's hot. We know that. I'm not going to mess around on this, Celie. I want to take him to the emergency room."

"He has an ear infection," a young male intern told them an hour and a half later. "But no sign of any other problem. His throat's fine, and his chest. I can prescribe an antibiotic, and you can give him some medicine for the pain. He'll start to feel a lot happier as soon as it kicks in."

"That's all it is?" Nick said. "Those are pretty common in babies, right?"

"A lot of babies are prone to ear infections, yes."

"That's great. That's— You don't know how much of a relief this is!"

Celie watched the concern ebb rapidly from Nick's

face and her heart turned over. He might not want the responsibility and commitment of adopting Carter, but no one could say he was taking this weekend lightly.

She wondered how easy he'd find it to hand the baby back to Ellen on Monday. Maybe he wouldn't be able to do it after all....

Searching in the baby change bag they'd brought with them, she found a tiny bottle of baby pain medication that Ellen had packed, and they filled the dropper to the right level and squirted it into Carter's mouth as soon as the doctor had left the cramped treatment room. Then they drove directly to a drugstore to pick up the baby's prescription antibiotic.

Carter remained fretful all the way home, but by the time they'd strapped him into the high chair Nick had bought, given him his first dose of pretty pink medicine, and warmed a jar of apricot puree by standing it in hot water for a few minutes, he'd quietened down. Celie touched her palm to his forehead. "He doesn't feel so warm anymore."

"Are you hungry, little guy?" Nick asked.

Carter was. He ate the whole jar of puree, and drank another half a bottle, snuggled in Nick's arms, while Celie wiped away the mess he'd made in his high chair. Next time she looked at the baby, he was asleep.

"So what do I do now?" Nick asked.

"Transfer him to the crib."

"What if he wakes up?"

"We'll cross that bridge when we come to it."

"Sounds like a plan."

Carefully, he got to his feet, lifted Carter so that his little head rested on the shoulder of the dark blue sweater. Then he tiptoed out of the room and up the stairs. Celie darted ahead of him to open the door and straighten Carter's bedding.

The baby stirred a little as Nick reached the crib, and so he swayed back and forth, murmuring, "Shh," in the hope that Carter would quickly settle again. He leaned his head closer to Carter's, making the dark hair color that they shared overlap and seem to merge, one big head, one little.

"How're you doing, kid?" he murmured. "Still asleep?"

Slowly and carefully he shifted, and glanced down at the baby with eyes that looked suddenly tired, in the dim bedroom. Tired blue eyes, pretty blue baby suit, the color of an airline pillow. Big dark head of hair, little dark hair of hair. They seemed to belong together. Like tulips and springtime. Like hotdogs and baseball.

My dream... Celie remembered.

She almost said it aloud, then realized that, no, this image hadn't come from a dream—or if it was a dream, it was one she'd only remembered as she sat in a business class airline seat watching Nick with a blue pillow in the crook of his arm.

Dream or reality, she didn't want to tell Nick about it right now. It seemed so long ago, but it was only a few weeks. So much had changed. In her heart, and everywhere.

She couldn't pretend to herself any more, the way she'd been pretending for weeks. Months, even. She'd fallen in love with Nick, and she wanted to belong in his arms the way Carter did, even though Nick couldn't see, yet, how completely Carter belonged.

Was it possible that he never would? Celie couldn't

believe that, not when she saw the tenderness in him. And would he ever feel about her the way she now knew she felt about him? She didn't know how to answer that question at all.

"Okay, crunch time," he whispered. "I'm going to lay him down. Watch how quickly he wakes up."

But Carter didn't wake up. The long wait in the hospital had tired him out. He put his head to the side, with his arm up beside it, and made little sucking sounds as if he didn't have a care in the world. Nick covered him, and both adults crept out of the room and didn't say a word all the way down the stairs.

Their silence came from differing motivations, Celie was certain.

When they reached the living room, Nick asked, "Do you think it's safe to speak now? Do you think we'll wake him up?"

"I think he's dead to the world, and dreaming about milk."

"Does this feel great, or what?" He grabbed her waist, laced his fingers together in the small of her back and waltzed her around the room.

She couldn't help laughing, giddy with so many mixed emotions. "What's this for?"

"Doesn't it feel like we achieved something, tonight? Doesn't this feel like a learning curve? We didn't have a clue, then we worked out he had a fever, we got it diagnosed, we gave him his medication, and now he's fine. And I'm starving. You never got that coffee, Celie. Do you want to eat?"

"Has Peg been cooking?"

"Let's go take a look." He let her go, way sooner than she wanted him to, but still not soon enough to leave her senses in peace.

They hung out in front of the freezer for several minutes, arguing about their choices, still a little giddy and light-headed with relief about Carter, until Nick finally said, "You know what? Let's cook. I feel like steak, and a beer, and music."

So they had a party for two.

Nick put on one of his favorite rock-and-roll CDs and opened two bottles of light beer. Celie wasn't a regular beer drinker, but tonight it felt right to have a cold bottle in her hand and to tip it to her lips every now and then, and gulp a big, fizzy mouthful.

Nick did the same, and she couldn't help watching the way his neck stretched up, the way his fingers gripped the bottle, the way he hung out by the stove flipping the sizzling meat on the griddle as he must have done back when Delaney's was just him and Sam.

Celie sliced an onion and Nick grilled that as well, pouring beer onto it for extra flavor and sweetness as it softened into golden-brown rings. She found potatoes and a bottle of Italian dressing in the pantry, sour cream and a bag of salad greens in the refrigerator. When they'd put it all together, they ate at the little café table in the kitchen, with the music still drifting through from the other room.

They talked about Carter, about Sam and Marisa, about movies and books and TV. They didn't talk about restaurant openings or advertising campaigns or Delaney's profit margin on appetizers.

"Want another beer?" Nick asked, when they'd finished eating.

"No, thanks." Celie smiled at him, feeling as if her bones were melting. And her boundaries. "Not a good idea," she said. "One's always enough for me."

One beer.

One man.

Nick.

She couldn't remember, anymore, why she'd fought the idea for so long. What was that about boundaries? Why did they need to exist, when so much else was more important?

"I'd suggest dancing," Nick answered, "only I don't think that would be a good idea, either."

It would be a wonderful idea. Nick just hadn't realized it yet.

"Why didn't you call the nanny agency and get a proper replacement, Nick?" Celie asked him.

He looked surprised at the apparent change of subject. "I wanted someone I could trust."

"You trust me to help you with Carter, but you don't trust me to dance with?"

She watched his face, her eyes daring him to look away. The table was small. Very small. She leaned a little closer, knowing that if he did the same, they'd easily be able to touch.

"That's about right," he answered. His gaze still clashed with hers, like twin ribbons of smoke mingling together.

"And do you trust yourself?" she asked.

"No. I really, really don't trust myself."

"Good." She stood up and leaned across the table, deliberately provocative in her pose. "We can work with that, I think." She spoke with a brisk, secretarial efficiency, mocking the professional relationship they'd had for eight long months, playing with it, daring him to retreat into it.

"Celie…" he began.

But her name disappeared into a breathy silence, brushed from his mouth by her kiss.

Chapter Eight

Celie had definitely done this on purpose. Nick knew it, but the knowledge didn't do a thing to dam back the power of his response.

She'd stretched across the table, with her arms folded across her body, just below her breasts. The loosely gathered neckline of her patterned pastel top had fallen open, and he'd caught a sensational and perfectly staged glimpse of satiny, shadowy skin, virginal white lace cut very low and two rounded shapes that he wanted instantly to touch and hold and kiss.

Before he could move a muscle, except to say her name, she'd stood up and leaned even closer, to take the kiss she wanted in the same way she might have plucked a bottle of correction fluid from his desktop.

Mine, thanks, and I need it.

Now. Because I'm very efficient, and when I've made a decision, I don't waste time.

It was a very short kiss. He closed his eyes, ready to taste and explore, but after one warm, moist moment of pressure, her mouth went away again. A growl of disappointment escaped from his throat and he opened his eyes, just in time to see her fingers slide along his jaw and her neat, curvy rear end slide into his lap. How had she moved around the table that fast?

"Celie…" he said, again.

This time the kiss didn't stop. He sat back, with his arms wrapped loosely around her body and gave himself to the hungry pressure of her mouth. The touch of her fingers on his jaw, like braided silk, sent him near crazy.

Don't move, the fingers seemed to say. We're keeping you right here as long as we want you. We'll be gentle about it, but you're not going anywhere.

Fine by him. There was nowhere he wanted to go. He loved that Celie had taken the initiative. He loved the small, hot flame of determination he sensed in her. He loved the way she was defying her own inexperience, pushing her own boundaries.

Her butt settled deeper into his lap, and the pressure and heat began to build. He raised his hands to her shoulders and pulled her closer, deepening the kiss she'd started, intensifying the strength of what they shared. In a minute, she wouldn't know what had hit her, and it heated his blood still further to imagine how she might respond to that.

How would she sound? How would she move?

There was a bow at the peasant-style gathered neckline of her top. He pulled on it and it unfastened. The gathers let go, and he slid the top off her shoulders and down her arms, until the neckline clung precariously to the soft jut of her breasts. He buried his face there, the low-cut lace bra giving him plenty of skin to taste. He felt her arch and gasp. Her fingers left his jaw and dug into his shoulders, and her breathing grew ragged as he clawed at her bra and freed her from it.

"Beautiful," he whispered.

She tried to kiss him again, but he wouldn't let her. Pressing his fingertips to her lips, he focused his full attention on her breasts, running the hardened tip of his tongue around the edge of each nipple, at the point where rosy-pink areola gave way to the paler color of her skin. The already peaked crests furled even tighter and he drew them into his mouth, pulling hard.

She slid off his lap, and he thought, no, she can't! She's stopping this? Now?

But she wasn't stopping anything. She only wanted more. Dragging him to his feet, she lifted the waistband of his sweater and pulled it up beneath his arms. He took control, drew the garment over his head and flung it aside.

"Much better," she said, still in that same efficient, secretarial tone that drove him wild because he'd been hearing it for months and he'd never realized how erotic and sensual it would sound in this context. She spread her palms across his bare chest and threaded her fingers through the silky hair that grew there. "How long have you been using the gym equipment?"

"Wh—?" Was she making small talk, at a time like this? "Um, okay, the stuff upstairs, a couple of years," he answered, bowing to her interrogation. His wits felt totally unraveled. "I've been going to various gyms since I was twenty."

"I like the results. They don't quite show up so much under your suits. I hadn't realized. Impressive, but not too extreme. Very touchable.'' She dropped her tone to a low purr. ''Very kissable.''

''I guess— Ahh…!'' He dragged in a long hiss of breath as she trailed her mouth from the base of his throat to his navel, letting her hot breath push on his skin.

She had her hands on his hips and was going even lower, toward the snap fastening. The zipper. The fly. He longed to release each of them for her, but if they got to that point, there'd be no turning back.

No turning back.

Sounded great.

Sounded perfect.

Sounded *essential,* his body said.

Boundaries, Nick, said a different part of him. What about boundaries? Why are you here? Why are you letting this happen? How are you going to deal with each other from now on, if it does? She's your executive assistant, not your executive lover.

He wanted to run his fingers through her hair and anchor her there. He wanted to close his eyes and find out what she planned to do to him, and how she planned to do it. How would efficient, capable Cecilia Rankin get from A to B on this particular journey?

But he knew he had to take control of himself, of this whole situation, before it sent them both over a cliff that they'd never be able to claw their way back up.

He gritted his teeth. ''Stop, Celie.''

Her arms wrapped around his thighs and she rolled her head to the side, so that her cheek was pressed into his hip bone. She looked up at him. Her hair was glossy and messy and wild around her face, and her smoky eyes were like black jewels.

"Okay, I've stopped," she said. "Wanna take off your jeans?"

"Yes. No. *Yes,* I want to, but— You know that. But— When did you get this wicked? No," he corrected himself quickly. "Don't answer that. Just…" He reached for her arms and unwound them from his thighs, feeling her trail her fingers deliberately across the knotted muscles she encountered.

He captured the fingers in his hands and pulled her up. She whipped her body against him on the way, and came to rest with her breasts, naked and warm and seeming fuller than they'd been half an hour ago, pressing into his chest. A shudder of intense desire rippled through him and he had to bite the inside of his cheeks as a distraction.

"Okay," he said. "Let's talk about this."

"Let's not," she whispered, sashaying her hips slowly from side to side.

"I'm not going through with it. We can't. There are so many reasons why this is a bad idea, that I don't even know where to start."

"I'll settle for three."

"Three what?"

"Three reasons," she repeated. "You said you didn't know where to start. So start with three."

"Celie…"

She mimed getting a notebook and pen out of a nonexistent pocket and smirked at him with a mouth swollen from kissing. "I'm ready to take dictation, sir."

"When did you get like this?" he asked, shaking his head in disbelief.

"Someday I might try to pinpoint that for myself,

because you're right, it's an interesting question, but right now I'm ready to hear reason number one."

"Reason number one," he echoed. "It's almost midnight. Morning is seven hours away."

"So?"

"The rest of our lives is seven hours away. I'm not taking you to bed for an hour of heaven, when that's incompatible with everything that kicks into gear again seven hours from now. Reason number two, I have some pretty important stuff to think about in my life right now, and if we sleep together, you'll want to have an input in all of that. I'll probably even want you to have an input. But that wouldn't be fair or right. To you or me or anyone. Reason number three…" He paused for a moment.

"Reason number three?" Celie prompted, pretending she hadn't been one single bit convinced by reasons one and two, even though, reluctantly, she had.

"Reason number three, Carter is crying. I can hear him. Listen."

After a few seconds of listening, Celie could hear him, too. "I guess the pain medication wore off," she said. "It's been four hours since we were at the hospital."

"I wonder if he's feverish again."

"We should check."

"I'll check," Nick told her, in a tone she didn't want to question.

Yes, Mr. Delaney, sir, she thought.

He reached for his sweater, dropped on the floor, and put it on, not seeming to care that it was inside out. Before Celie had even managed to move, he'd left the kitchen. It seemed cold without him, although the spring night was mild. The freezer and refrigerator hummed in the sudden quiet, making a background to the sound of Nick's feet on the stairs, and the fainter drone of the baby's cries.

Celie cupped her hands over her breasts. They felt tender and sensitized, their nipples still hard from the friction of Nick's mouth. Something pulsed low inside her as she remembered how it had felt to be in such intimate contact with his body. To be left like this felt like having a warm, protective cloak ripped roughly from her form.

She found her bra and her top and put them on quickly, in the hope that the intensity of memory and sensation would be masked by the layers of fabric, but it didn't really work that way. She knew she'd relive this past half hour in her memory, and in her body, for months.

Upstairs, she heard Carter's crying intensify, and Nick's deep voice didn't seem to soothe him. He needed more pain medication, but she remembered how tricky they'd found it at the hospital to squirt the liquid into his mouth. Then, the task had required both of them, and this time wouldn't be any different. Nick and Carter needed her help.

When Celie reached Nick's room, she found him holding Carter across one hip while he frantically rummaged in the baby change bag with his free hand. He saw her come in, and asked, "Where the heck did we put the medication? Do you remember?"

"In one of the side pockets, I think."

"Right. Which one?"

"Let me take a look. You can't do it one-handed. You look like you're about to drop him."

"Maybe that's what he's trying to tell me. Is that what you're trying to tell me, baby boy?" he crooned, standing straight and getting Carter snuggled more comfortably against him.

Celie searched the side pockets of the bag, and found the small brown glass bottle they were looking for. "Sit him in your arms on the bed," she suggested. "If he turns his head away while we're doing this, he'll get sticky stuff all over his face and we'll have to start again."

"Okay, here we go." Nick sat on the bed and positioned Carter in the crook of his arm. "He does feel hot again, and his ear is red. No wonder he's cranky, poor guy. I hope the antibiotic kicks in soon."

Celie squirted in the contents of the dropper. Carter made a face and tried to spit it back out, but almost all of it went down his throat, thank goodness.

"Around twenty minutes until it starts working," Nick said. He made a fist to cover a yawn. "I'll stay up with him. You go to bed, Celie."

"I'd rather keep you guys company."

"I'd rather you went to bed." He looked up at her, his gaze steady.

"Is that because you don't trust what might happen with the two of us, once the baby's asleep and lying in his crib?" she asked, as cool as he was.

"You got it in one."

"Just checking."

"Not going to talk me out of it?"

"Want me to?"

He closed his eyes and pressed his lips together. When he spoke, his voice was like gravel churning in the barrel of a concrete mixer. "You know what I want," he said. His eyes were still closed. "Don't push us into the same discussion, all over again. It's late, Celie, and my sense of perspective could turn into a pumpkin at midnight, not to mention my control. In the meantime, Carter could easily wake again at four. Get some sleep.''

"Now, why do you suppose I did that, baby boy?" Nick muttered to Carter, once it became clear that Celie had gone to her room, just as he'd asked her to, and wasn't coming back. "Why did I send a willing woman away, when I'm so attracted to her I'm going cross-eyed over it?''

He rocked the baby in his arms, and got only some diminishing fussing sounds for an answer. The sole light in the room came from a night-light plugged into a socket low on the wall, and the atmosphere was peaceful and quiet.

Nice.

He should have a rocking chair. It wasn't all that comfortable perching on the edge of the bed, trying to keep this to-and-fro motion going. His neck and shoulders ached.

"Go to sleep, Carter," he told his nephew, but the baby's brown eyes stared up at him, interested and alert. "Oh, you're waiting to hear my theory about what's going on? Is that it?" he asked. "Yeah, I guess you have a vested interest.''

He smiled at the baby, because it was pretty hard not to, and Carter smiled back.

"All right," Nick said. "My theory. It's simple, I guess. Celie and I have both tapped into a whole lot of emotions we never needed to have before. Discovering that you existed was incredible. Seems like your existence should be the end of the story, you know, but it's not. Is this making any sense?''

Carter smiled again. He'd started to look a little

sleepy, and he wasn't crying anymore. Cautiously, Nick eased off his shoes and swiveled his legs onto the bed. If he lay with Carter in the crook of his arm for a few minutes, and covered the two of them with his light quilt, to create a cocoon of warmth, the baby would probably get to sleep faster.

"I've only ever slept with a woman when it was simple," he told his nephew once they were both settled in the new position. "And when we both had a clear understanding of what we wanted and how far it could go. The thing is, sex is like some kind of mind-altering drug. You don't need to know that yet, little buddy, but one day you probably will. It can distort your perceptions. It can make you think that you feel things when you don't, especially when you're pretty inexperienced, like Celie is."

Carter yawned.

"I know," Nick said. He yawned, also. "You wanted the short version and you're not getting it. Don't worry. I'm nearly done. What it all adds up to, is that I'm the one with the power and the control, and that's a responsibility. To you. To Ellen. To Sam. To Celie. Basically, I can't create expectations in any of you that I can't follow through on, in the cold light of day. All of you deserve better than that. Celie, especially…"

He closed his eyes, and tried to come out with the right words to describe to Carter exactly what was so special about Celie, why she deserved such special treatment. The baby warmed his arm. His big brown eyes had drifted shut, now, and his breathing had gotten soft and regular and slow. But before Carter fell asleep, Nick had to tell him the rest of his feelings about Celie.

He'd get there in a minute. He really would. He'd just think about it for a little longer before he spoke....

Something was making the bed rock, and someone was making sounds—odd, happy little sounds with no words attached. The room was light, but Nick decided he had no reason to wake up. The bed rocked more, and the creature making the odd, wordless noises sounded very pleased with itself.

Then came a thump and a cry and a shocked exclamation in a female voice that Nick recognized. His eyes flew open, and there was Celie. She had Carter scooped up in her arms and she was holding him close, kissing him and soothing him. He was crying with the energy of an express train sounding its whistle as it rocketed toward a station.

Nick swore. "He fell off the bed? I must have gone to sleep last night with him still in my arms. I'm a heavy sleeper. He woke up and started playing and I didn't realize what was happening."

"He didn't hit his head," Celie said. "He went feet first, and thumped backward onto his bottom. His head would have hit the ground next, but I got to him just in time."

"Thanks. Major, serious thanks, Celie. You heard him from your room?"

"I heard him start to play, and then when I didn't hear any response from you, I figured you were still asleep. I thought I'd get him out of his crib and take him downstairs, let you sleep a little longer. Shh, baby," she told Carter. "You had a scare, didn't you? But you're okay."

"Not sure if I am," Nick said. "My heart's going

a mile a minute. I'm not used to treating my bed as if it's a cliff edge.''

''There's a lot to think of with a baby,'' Celie agreed.

They both heard an extra significance in both statements. In their lives, right now, beds were like cliff edges, and babies needed a lot of thought. Nick saw Celie's reaction in the way her face suddenly changed, going sober and thoughtful.

Yeah, there was a lot to think of.

Like Carter's whole future.

And there was the other thing, too.

Last night.

Him and Celie, locked together.

The huge thing that had almost happened between them. The thing she'd tried shamelessly to engineer, with a combination of seductive secretarial efficiency and shy wickedness that made him throb and pulse as soon as he thought about it.

He could tell by the way she held her body, and by the way she looked at him, that it was still on her mind, but he couldn't tell how she felt about it.

How she felt was irrelevant, probably.

Only one of them needed the certainty that it couldn't go anywhere, and that it mustn't happen again.

''I'd better call Ellen this morning, with a report,'' he said, clawing his way back up the cliff edge to a safer subject. He paused briefly in his thought track to contemplate, with a degree of shock, the fact that he considered Carter a safer subject than Celie, now. When had that happened?

''I wonder if she tried calling here last night while we were at the hospital.'' He went on quickly. ''Or if she got too caught up with her new grandchild to feel concerned.''

''You'll tell her about the ear infection?''

''When she gets back. I don't want to worry her. He seems fine this morning, and he slept beyond when the pain medication would have worn off. Maybe the antibiotic has started working.''

''He's due for another dose over breakfast.''

The three of them ate together in the kitchen, with the morning sun making the room bright. The May day had already shaped up to be gorgeous, clear skied and around seventy degrees. A week from now, summer would probably kick in, early as usual and unmistakably different from spring, with its high humidity and low, pale skies. This day deserved savoring.

Nick called his brother after breakfast, and Sam said he'd drop over later and come to the park with them. Hearing Nick's half of the conversation, Celie could tell that Sam was eager to meet his nephew, but even less able than Nick to contemplate the adoption that Ellen Davis wanted.

After the phone call, and still lingering over coffee, pastries and the Saturday newspapers, Celie and Nick took Carter out to Nick's large, landscaped wooden deck that jutted into the south-facing rear yard. The baby sat on a blanket in the sunshine, propped up with pillows. He played with his baby gym while the two adults finished off their lazy brunch.

Playing with a baby gym was pretty exhausting, apparently. After a while, Carter sagged into a horizontal position and did a couple of cute little practice flips from his tummy to his back, and the other way around, then he started a kind of crying that, even to

Nick and Celie's inexperienced ears, said very clearly, "I'm sleepy."

"I'll take him up," Celie offered.

She took a while to change his diaper and get him settled, and when she came downstairs again, she discovered that Sam had arrived.

He and Nick were in Nick's study, and she only needed to hear a few phrases with the word *lawyer* through the half-open door to realize that they were talking about Sam's divorce, and that the conversation was private. She went back upstairs, chose a murder mystery from the bookshelf in her room and slipped out to the deck to read it and soak up some more sun.

Carter slept until noon.

"Wow!" Sam said, when Nick brought the baby downstairs, just as Celie came in from the deck.

He repeated the word, looking very emotional. "Wow..." His jaw worked for a few moments, and he pressed his lips together hard. He'd lost weight in recent weeks, Celie realized, and since he'd had very little to spare in the first place, he almost looked gaunt. If Nick had been worried about him before the official separation, she could see he was even more worried about him now.

With the close bond that the two brothers had, which would be made even closer with Carter's arrival in their lives, she felt out of place. She wasn't really safe here anymore, for all sorts of reasons. Sam must be wondering why Nick had called on her as a backup nanny, instead of going with someone else from the agency. She didn't want him asking any tough questions, or saying anything to Kyla.

"Here. Hold him, bro," Nick said, obviously wanting to give his brother something safe and concrete to focus on. He held the baby out.

"I don't know how," Sam answered.

"Here's a little secret. You learn. Much faster than you think you will. Do you hear the way I'm giving you advice? After, what, twenty-one hours, I'm an expert!"

"I'm going to hold you to that claim, Nick," Celie announced, stepping forward with the murder mystery still in her hand.

"How do you mean?" He looked a little alarmed.

"If you're an expert, then you don't need me anymore. We got through the hard part last night, I'm sure. You and Sam want to hang out together, doing guy stuff with Carter, right? He's more than ready to learn to swing a baseball bat, for example." The jokey approach didn't quite work, so she stopped and tried something else. "And I'm…you know…I have things I should get done at home, before Monday."

"Washing your hair?" Nick suggested, with a glint in his eye.

"Yes, that." She met the glint with defiance. "Can I borrow this book?" She held it up.

"As long as you promise to bring it back if I need it urgently, like, say, at midnight tonight."

"Carter's not going to wake up tonight. And even if he does, you'll know what he wants as well as I would. Maybe Sam could stay over."

"I have things to get done by Monday, too," Sam said, and frowned. "My lawyer says I should go through every—" He stopped, obviously remembering that Celie was in the room. "Tell you in a minute, Nick. Celie, I don't want to…uh…bore you with this."

"That's fine, Sam. I understand."

She hurried upstairs to repack her overnight bag, and Nick appeared in the spare room doorway just as she was ready. At the sight of him, her heart jumped in her chest like a pancake flipping. He hadn't shaved this morning, and he wore a similar casual outfit to yesterday's—jeans with a gray T-shirt on top. They couldn't look at each other, even across a spacious room, without feeling the pull.

"Thanks for staying over," he said.

"Uh…yeah, but I realized you and Sam needed some time."

"That's about leaving, not about staying over."

"I was glad to stay over, and I'd have stayed on if Sam hadn't come to keep you company. You really don't have to thank me."

"I want to," he said.

"What if I said I'd rather you didn't?"

"I wouldn't take any notice. These hours will show up on your pay stub, too, by the way."

"No." She felt her cheeks heat up, and her heart stopped flipping and started to sink. "I don't want that. I absolutely don't want that, Nick!"

It hurt that he could propose to pay her for helping him with Carter. She knew why it hurt, and she knew why he'd proposed it. They each viewed things so differently now, and Nick didn't show any sign that he believed he should change.

"I know you don't want it," he said, without smiling. "But it's not up to you. It's up to me. Let me carry your bag to the car, and then I'll see you on Monday afternoon."

"See you Monday afternoon, bro," Sam said, climbing into his car. "Good luck with the rest of the weekend."

"So now it's just you and me, kid," Nick said to the baby, after Sam had gone.

Sam had stayed for one of Peg's freezer meals, so it was getting late in baby land, and Carter would soon be ready for bed. He'd had his antibiotic, he didn't seem in need of any more pain medication. So what else was there? A bath. A diaper change. A change of outfit, because this one had pureed carrot all over it. Ellen said he liked a bedtime story, too. He seemed amazingly bright for five and a half months, and beautifully engaged with the world.

A feeling of pride stirred inside Nick, like a creature waking from winter hibernation, and it scared him. He wanted to feel the right feelings for Carter, but he wanted them carefully measured. Sam had said something tonight, in reference to his marriage, but it resonated with Nick's feelings about parenthood, too.

"Do you ever wonder if Mom and Dad were too late when they took us on? If there were some lessons about love that it was already too late for us to learn? And some bad lessons they could never undo?"

Yeah, Nick had wondered that.

He'd been thinking a lot about what Ellen had said about Jane and their birth mother, and for the first time he'd actually tried to bring the memories back, instead of blocking them out. There still weren't many. There was still nothing concrete. But all of it had the same flavor—chaos and unpredictability. The message lay deep in his bones that safety could turn to danger, approval to anger, and pleasure to loss, without warning, in mere seconds.

Love was the most unpredictable element of all. It

could wear so many different faces. It could be manic and exuberant. It could vanish without trace. It could be frightening, and sad, and impossible to bear.

Mom and Dad had spent years showing him and Sam that love wasn't any of those things, but, no, they hadn't fully succeeded. Sam had chosen the superficial, shallow face of love, and it had let him down. Nick wanted to wait until love came in a neat package, that wouldn't explode in his face. Surely that wasn't wrong. Surely that was possible.

He picked the baby up and took him upstairs to the bathroom. Since Carter had been sick last night, Nick and Celie hadn't had a chance to bathe him together. Nick realized that, beyond the basic principle of getting the kid's clothes off, getting him wet, getting him dry and getting him dressed again, he had no idea about how to do this.

He got to the bathroom, surveyed the utter lack of baby bathing equipment and laughed at himself and Carter in the mirror.

"Will you look at us?" he said. "What are we going to do, little guy? Can I put you in the basin? Can I use regular soap, or is that bad for your skin? Will you forgive me if this is the weirdest bath you've ever had? Yeah, you will, won't you? You're pretty tolerant, and pretty flexible. You're totally cool."

Fifteen minutes later, with a towel tucked into the back of his jeans, water all over the bathroom floor, and the slipperiest, smiliest baby in the entire universe tenuously grasped in his arms, Nick lifted him up, blew a big raspberry on his wet tummy and told him with an odd, tight feeling in his chest, "You know what? I'm not looking forward to Monday."

Chapter Nine

Right up until when it happened, Celie didn't believe that Nick would really do it. She didn't believe he'd just hand Carter back to Ellen Davis on Monday as if the assignment was over and nothing in his feelings had changed.

Even on Friday night, he seemed to have gotten so much warmer with Carter, and so much more comfortable about their relationship. On Saturday, he'd told Sam, sounding very complacent about it, that he was an expert. Despite her hurt over Nick's insistence on paying her extra for what she'd done, Celie had spent the rest of the weekend with a little smile on her face, imagining the way his feelings for his nephew would deepen even further, especially without her around to complicate the picture.

All through Monday morning in her office, every time the phone rang, she kept thinking it would be Nick, with some urgent instructions for her.

"I've decided to keep Carter, and I need you to

research Ohio adoption regulations,'' he'd say. Or at the very least, ''I won't be in to the office today, so you'll have to reschedule a couple of things. Ellen and I need to talk about plans. I want to have a greater involvement in Carter's life.''

But he didn't call, and she got through the work on her desk, liaised with various corporate executives in various different Delaney's divisions on his behalf, and then began stalling on her lunch break, because she didn't want to leave the building until he'd arrived.

He appeared at one-fifteen. ''I would have gotten here a lot sooner, only Ellen's flight was delayed.''

''So what happened?'' Celie asked. ''How did it go?''

''It was just some mechanical thing that turned out to be a false alarm.''

''No, I mean, with Carter, and Ellen.''

''I told her about the ear infection, but she wasn't fazed. Her daughter and new granddaughter are both fine, and she had a great weekend.''

''And where's Carter now?''

He looked at her. ''Heading back in Ellen's car to Cleveland,'' he said, exaggerating the patience in his tone. ''You knew that was the plan, Celie.''

''Yes, but...'' Her eyes suddenly began to sting. ''Plans can change.''

Feelings can change.

Everything can change.

She didn't waste her energy on saying the words aloud.

Nick didn't answer, just strode toward his office. In the doorway, he paused. ''I'll need you to make some phone calls. I want you to prepare a list of domestic staffing agencies in the Cleveland area that handle nannies and cleaners. I've drafted an outline of the requirements. You could look over it for me, and see if there's anything I've missed. I showed it to Ellen, and she thought it was fine, but you have experience in personnel and staffing issues that she lacks.''

''Of course,'' Celie answered him.

She hadn't used such a wooden, efficient, impersonal tone toward him since her first week in the job. In nine months as her boss, he'd never reduced her to tears, but there was a first time for everything, and as far as crying went, this could be it.

''When do you want the information, and when do you need the draft back?'' she asked.

''As soon as you can, on both. I stalled on all of this last week, but Ellen needs the support, and I want to get it in place. I'll go up there for interviews as soon as they're scheduled.''

''Will Sam—?''

''Sam's leaving this to me. Just as you will, Celie, apart from handling the things I ask you to do.''

''I understand.''

''It's nothing personal…''

''It never is,'' she dared to say, and saw his jaw tighten.

''That's just as it should be, in this environment,'' he answered. ''We've both been in danger of forgetting that, and it's time we got back into line. Am I clear?''

''Very.''

''Good.''

She managed to hold the tears back until she got home to her apartment that night, but then they came flooding out. If Nick couldn't take Carter fully into his life, then there was no place in his life for herself, either.

Celie couldn't put it into words any better than that, and she couldn't make sense of why it should be true. She just knew that it was.

Loving him the way she did, she needed him to love Carter as a son, and it didn't look as if that was ever going to happen.

The apartment seemed to share her feelings. The clock was surely ticking slower, and the water for her pasta took a long time to reach the boil. That night, she had a long, sketchy series of dreams about packing, full of old-fashioned steamer trunks and modern file boxes and circled classifieds in the newspaper.

She didn't know what they meant, and couldn't come up with a positive interpretation. The Dream Stitcher seemed to be helping her with the packing at one point, folding fabric and laying it in piles, so she asked her, "Am I losing my job? Am I leaving here?"

"Kyla will blossom with the change. Don't worry."

"I'm happy for Kyla," Celie answered, with an edge of sarcasm in her tone. The cryptic answer was annoying, to say the least! She glared at the Dream Stitcher, but the Dream Stitcher only smiled and went on folding.

There was an old-fashioned paper luggage label on the windowsill the following morning, and a note from Anna Jardine in her mailbox that same afternoon.

"Here's my phone number," it read. "I'd love for

you to give me a call, and maybe we can get together. I want an update on the baby in your dreams!''

Celie wished she had a more positive report to give.

Nick had both a nanny and a cleaner for Ellen Davis interviewed and selected by the end of the week, due to start work the following Monday.

Meanwhile, his mom and dad had come up from Florida for their usual summer in Ohio. They would stay part of the time with Nick, part of the time with Sam, and the rest they'd spend in their little lakefront cabin in northern Ohio, on a half acre of beautiful forested land. They'd structured their lives this way for several years, now, since his dad's retirement as an executive with a pharmaceutical company.

Nick presented his and Sam's decision on how to fit Carter into their lives as a fait accompli, and they didn't question it. They wanted to see the baby, so he arranged with Ellen that they'd make a visit on their way through to the cabin on the weekend. When they reached the cabin, they called him and reported that it had been a very pleasant couple of hours.

''The baby is adorable,'' his mom said. ''And Mrs. Davis seems so competent! I hope I'm even half as good, if I'm ever a grandparent.''

His parents had never put any pressure on Nick or Sam to marry and produce children. It was another area in which they believed in stepping back and letting their boys make their own choices.

Nick had always loved them for this, as he loved them for so many things, but on Sunday night, after he'd put down the phone at the end of their call, he was flooded with an irrational wish that this time, just for once, they'd behave unfairly.

He wanted them to get over-the-top emotional, apply unreasonable pressure, express an illogical opinion that he didn't agree with so he could do the exact opposite. He wanted them to blackmail him emotionally with some elaborate fantasy about piles of gifts for granchildren under the Christmas tree, or teaching a little person to fish off the cabin's dock, so he could tell them ''No way!'' or, alternatively, capitulate and yell, ''Okay, if it's that important to you, I'll do it!''

None of this made any sense, so he ignored it.

More than two weeks passed—difficult weeks full of petty problems that he'd usually hand immediately to Celie and forget all about.

Why had that strategy suddenly stopped working? Maybe because they'd gotten so stiff and distant and awkward with each other. Angry, both of them. Full of the usual potent chemistry, despite all his attempts to ignore it. It was quite clear that she wished it would go away, as well.

He kept wanting to justify himself to her, and that made him even angrier. He wanted to tell her the details every time he phoned Ellen to get an update on Carter, and on how the new cleaner and nanny were working out.

Every time, however, he resisted and said nothing about it. Let Celie think anything she wanted. If she thought he never called Cleveland, so much the better. This was his personal life, and not her concern.

''Could you copy this report ready for the meeting this afternoon?'' he asked her on an unseasonably hot Thursday morning, nearly three weeks after his weekend with Carter.

That long?

Yes, three weeks, tomorrow.

Not that he was counting, or anything.

The air-conditioning was locked in a losing battle with the sun streaming through the big windows of his office, putting him in a bad mood. He'd been watching the hot patches of yellow light slowly traveling across his floor for half the morning, no doubt fading the plush carpet. In the afternoon, the sun would disappear and his office would be cool again, thank heaven. Maybe then he'd actually get something done.

Meanwhile, he considered calling building maintenance to get them to crank up the air-conditioning. So what if everyone else started shivering? His was the executive office. Why should he swelter in it?

"The copy machine is playing up," Celie told him, in answer to his request about the report. The information provided the icing on the cake to his mood.

He knew Ellen Davis didn't have air-conditioning at her place. How would she handle Carter in the heat? How had she handled all those other babies and toddlers and big kids? She was amazing. He'd been thinking about it all morning. So many of his thoughts seemed to arrow directly back to Carter now, and if they didn't, they arrowed back to Celie instead.

"The technician's working on it," she explained.

"Great!" he said, through clenched teeth.

"Anything else?" she asked.

"You tell me. What else isn't working?"

"Nothing, as far as I'm aware."

"Nothing's working?"

"Everything's working, Nick," Celie clarified patiently, still standing in front of his desk. "Nothing else is *not* working."

All their exchanges seemed to be like this, just lately, she thought.

Awkward.

Full of misinterpretations.

Every day, she was on the verge of tears.

She went back to her own office, bringing the report he wanted copied. She'd get it done as soon as the technician reported success with the machine. Meanwhile, she'd make the arrangements for yet another trip away with her boss, scheduled for next week. It would be their first since California, and she wasn't looking forward to it.

The phone rang, and she recognized Ellen Davis's voice on the line at once. "Is Nick available?"

"I'll put you right through, Ellen." Celie had made an executive decision that her boss would always be available for his nephew's foster mother, and Nick hadn't questioned it.

As a way to smooth the path of their relationship, it felt like such a small thing to do, though, and she was sure the Dream Stitcher must be disappointed in her. She was disappointed in herself. If you loved a man and he didn't even listen to you, what did that say about the way he felt? Nothing that counted as good news.

In his baking hot office, Nick took the call from Carter's foster mom. "Everything okay, Ellen?" he said.

She'd called a couple of times in the middle of the day like this, but only when it was important. Two weeks ago, she'd needed him to find the repeat order on the antibiotic prescription, which he'd forgotten to give her, and one day last week she'd told him that the nanny had called in sick, and asked what he wanted her to do when that happened. Should she call the agency to get a substitute?

"Of course," he'd told her. "You don't need my permission on that."

"No, I know. But I mean, do I have to do that?" Ellen was more than happy to manage on her own, she'd assured him. "Uh, no, it's not totally okay, Nick," she said now, her voice husky with reluctance.

Nick's heart did a sideways kind of kick that made him feel queasy. "What's up? What's happened?"

"I'm sorry. This nanny thing isn't working out. Or the cleaner. They're sweet, both of 'em. They're trying. But I'm not used to having people around the house taking orders from me. I'm trying to get your money's worth. But I'm too uncomfortable with it."

"We can interview some more people. Maybe it's a personality thing."

"No. It's not that. It's just not what I'm used to. And yet I know you're right. I'm seventy next month. I'm not the right person to care for Carter on my own. Looking a few years down the track, it's only going to get harder. And then last night my daughter Lisa came for a visit with her two kids. They live in Maine."

"So the house is crowded, I guess," he put in, trying to be helpful.

He was still waiting for some punch line about Carter, impatient for it, sweating for it, stomach roiling. Didn't sound like the baby was in the hospital or anything, so Nick's heart had started beating again, almost the way it was supposed to. But he knew that more was coming. His scalp prickled.

"Well, she's come up with a plan that might make

things work out best for all of us,'' Ellen said. ''Lisa and Jane grew up together, on and off. Lisa's just two years older, and they were pretty close for a while. Her own girls are three and five now. She called her husband first thing this morning, after we discussed it, and he's agreed.''

''Agreed to what?''

Ellen sketched out the plan in six words, and Nick dropped the phone, too shocked to speak.

When Celie went in to Nick's office some minutes later, to report that the photocopy machine wasn't fixed yet, and to give him another sheaf of papers that he needed, she found him still sitting there, and one look at his face told her there was a problem.

''What's happened?'' she blurted. ''Oh, Nick!''

If he'd been looking at her, if he'd actually focused on her face, everything she felt would have been written there as plain as day, but he wasn't looking at her face, so she was safe. For the moment, at least.

He wasn't. He looked like a man with vertigo, teetering on the lip of a three-hundred-foot cliff.

''Ellen phoned,'' he said. ''Her daughter in Maine wants to adopt Carter.''

''Oh, Nick!'' Celie said again. Her vocabulary had left work early, apparently.

''I'm—'' He stopped, and shook his head.

''You don't want him to go so far away.'' That much was obvious.

''No.''

''And what does Ellen want?''

''The same as I want. What we all want. What's best for Carter.'' Nick stood up, his eyes unfocused, and began to pace, like a lion who would rip his cage apart with his bare claws if he had the power. "I've been kidding myself, Celie," he said at last.

I know.

"I thought we could make it work the way we had it set up." He went on. "But it's not going to, and now I have to choose between— I don't know if I can do this."

"Do what, Nick?"

"Make the right decision. Could I really be the best parent for him…?"

"Only if you want to be." She didn't even know if he was listening. "That's what he needs. All he needs. For you to *want* to be."

"…I don't think I could," he finished, his voice heavy.

He leaned onto his desk, closed his eyes and shook his head again, resting his weight on fingertips that soon went white with the pressure. Celie waited for a moment—waited for him to look up again, say something, look as if he remotely cared that she was here.

She debated going to him, putting her arms around him, soothing him with more words, pep-talking him into wanting Carter enough to get over all that held him back.

No.

She'd hurt herself enough already, with her involvement in Nick's life. She would have kept on hurting herself, too, if she'd thought it would do any good. For Carter. For Nick. But right now she didn't think it would.

"I'll be in my office if you need me," she finally told him.

"Yep. Thanks." His eyes were still closed.

* * *

Celie looked up at the sound of a rap on her open door, shortly before lunch, and the copy machine technician reported, "It's working fine, now. I replaced a couple of components."

"Do me a favor, don't tell me what they're called," she answered.

The technician laughed, rewarding the lame humor she'd struggled to find.

She picked up the report Nick had given her. "So I can...?"

"Yep. Go right ahead. Test it out."

She returned twenty minutes later, with the report already collated and bound and teetering in a big pile in her arms, ready for this afternoon's meeting. Putting the pile on her desk, she went to Nick's office, glad of the excuse to check up on him, but the office was empty.

Hot and empty.

She checked and discovered that somehow one of the two air-conditioning vents had gotten closed, possibly during a cleaner's recent visit, so she opened it again and felt a cool waft of air at once. That should help, hopefully by the time he got back.

If he got back. She had no idea where he'd gone. The bathroom? Or—?

"Celie?" Kyla said, just behind her. "He said to tell you he's left."

"Left?" She whirled around.

"For the day." Kyla spread her hands, and silver bracelets jingled on her wrist. "Doesn't know when he'll be back in."

Okay, what did that mean?

"That wasn't in the plan."

"Yeah, he looked a bit shaken up. Actually, a lot shaken up. Didn't slow down on his way out. He just told me Sam would have to handle the meeting." She frowned, then grinned wryly. "Whatever happened to the two cyber businessmen we used to work for, huh?"

"You think they've changed?" Celie asked.

"Don't you? I never thought Sam would be so racked by his divorce."

"I wish Nick would change," Celie blurted out.

"You don't think he has? You don't think it'll happen?"

"I think he'll tie himself in knots to make sure it doesn't happen, and you know what? I'm not sure— I'm really not sure—how much longer I can stand watching him do that."

"My lord, Celie, you're going to leave?" Kyla breathed.

"He keeps telling me not to…"

"You've gotten pretty open with each other, then, if you can talk on that level. I— Shoot, you know? I don't think Sam even remembers my name, half the time. I'm just the blonde in the sassy clothes who gets stuff done."

"Kyla, that's not true."

"It is at the moment. I happened to mention my daughter the other day and he gave me this look as if he'd forgotten I had one. I don't know why it even upsets me. But we're not talking about me. We're talking about you. Leaving. Do you really have to?"

"I didn't think I would ever leave for a reason like this."

"Oh, Celie!"

Her voice thickened with tears she absolutely refused to shed. "But I just don't think I can stick around watching him *not change,* Kyla. Not with the way I—the way I—"

"Feel about him. Okay." Kyla nodded slowly, with round eyes, and Celie knew she didn't need to get to the end of the sentence. The whole truth had to be written all over her face.

"Feel about him," she echoed, her voice sliding away into silence.

"Do you need me to handle your side of the meeting?" Kyla said.

She straightened her shoulders, steadied her jaw. "No, I'm fine. I am. I guess Nick will call me eventually, with an update on what's going on. Did he… uh…happen to mention whether it was personal?"

Kyla raised an expressive eyebrow. "His body language mentioned it," she drawled. "Even if *he* didn't. It was most definitely personal."

But that didn't tell Celie very much at all.

Chapter Ten

Nick didn't show up for the meeting, didn't call, and didn't show up for work the next day, either, although there was a terse list of instructions for Celie on her answering machine when she got into work that morning.

"And I haven't seen him since," she told Anna Jardine, on Saturday afternoon, when Anna and her darling little Maybelle came over for coffee.

"You're really concerned," Anna said.

"I just wish I knew what it meant. Is Ellen's daughter's adoption proceeding that fast? Is Carter going to Maine, and Nick has gone to Cleveland to say goodbye?"

"Maine isn't the end of the earth."

"It's too far."

"No hints about what's happening from our dear friend?"

"No, unfortunately." Celie frowned across at the mirror. In the afternoon light, it looked a little dusty.

"She's not being real helpful on this one, to be honest. She's still on about packing boxes and circling newspaper classifieds."

"Sounds like you'll be looking for a new apartment soon." Anna smiled, as if remembering a delicious secret, but Celie was too caught up in her concerns over Nick to question her on it.

She closed her eyes for a moment and shook her head. "No, I'll be looking for a new job," she said. "That has to be what the classifieds mean. Kyla asked me on Thursday if I was going to leave. I hadn't planned to. I don't want to. But I'm starting to think it's the only safe option. Especially if Nick just lets Carter go off to Maine."

Anna took a mouthful of her coffee and then smiled again. "Hasn't the Dream Stitcher convinced you yet that there's no such thing as a safe option?"

"Sometimes she's not nearly as clear as I want her to be!"

"Wait and see," Anna said. She picked her baby up and kissed her, her face masked by Maybelle's wobbly golden head.

"Tell me about what happened to you, Anna. What sequence of dreams did you have? How did they change you? How long did it take before everything got clear? I'd really like to know the whole story, if you don't mind telling it."

She needed a happy ending, right now, even if it belonged to someone else.

"I'd love to tell it!"

Celie drank some coffee and said, "I'm listening."

"Well, it all started when I was modeling," Anna began, but she didn't get any further than that.

Celie's phone rang, and she snatched it up with a prickle of intuition. "Nick?"

"How did you—? Never mind. I guess I should have gotten used to your psychic vibes, by now."

Celie didn't tell him that it was desperation not intuition that had made her say his name on this occasion.

"I'm in my car," he continued, "calling to see if you're home. Which you obviously are, along with your dream lady. Can I swing round to your place?"

"Please. I want to hear about—"

"I'll be there in five."

He got there in three. Anna had asked if she should continue her story, but Celie had told her, "I'm sorry. I don't think I could focus on it right now, after all."

"Of course you couldn't. I'll get Maybelle ready and we'll head out. Come over to my place next time? I'd love you to meet my husband."

"I'd like that."

"I'll call you, okay?"

Anna and Maybelle met Nick on his way up the stairs. Celie managed a vague introduction, and Anna pretended an urgent need to get going, which Celie was grateful for.

Nick looked different today. He filled her apartment with his presence, but that wasn't new. He would have filled it in just the same way months ago, if she'd ever had a reason to bring him here. So what was new?

The wide, teasing smile? The radiant energy? The sky-blue paint splotch on the back of his jeans? Celie saw the paint stain reflected in the mirror, as Nick faced her, and for some reason the mirror didn't look dusty anymore. Maybe the light had changed.

"I don't know where to start," Nick said. He paced. Like a lion in a cage. Like a man soothing a fussy baby, wrapped in a blanket the color of an airline pillow. "There's something I want to show you. Is that what we should do first?"

Celie laughed and spread her hands. "If you want."

She didn't know what might be coming. The weight had gone from his shoulders. He'd made a decision. And obviously he felt happy about that. Her heart began to beat faster, and she wondered if she would feel the same when he told her what the decision was.

"I like your apartment." He looked around at the mirror and the chandelier and the windowsill. "Hey, apartment, I like you. I don't usually talk to people's apartments, by the way, but in this case it seems appropriate." He said to Celie, "Does she ever reply?"

"Not in the daytime."

"Then maybe I'll have to come here at night." He didn't give her time to react to the line, or the way he'd delivered it, dropping his voice just a couple of notes. "Celie?"

"Yes?"

"Is there anything you need to grab? Your bag, or something? I want to get going. This seems like a pretty safe neighborhood, but I have a horse in the back seat of my car, and you never can tell."

"You have a horse?" She picked up her bag, while a giant's hand seemed to squeeze her lungs like wringing out a sponge. "I'm ready," she added vaguely.

"A toy. You'll see it in a minute."

He reached around and pulled the door closed behind them, and she felt the brush of his arm across her shoulder. She looked at him and her limbs froze in place. Love and wanting flooded her like an ocean wave, and her whole body tingled with the need to touch and hold him, to tell him everything she felt.

He nudged his hand into her lower back, and let it trail lower, like a caress, before he took it away again. "Come on."

"Is that what you wanted me to see?" she said. "The horse?"

"Nope. There's a lot more than that." He led the way down the stairs and she followed, her gaze catching on all the parts of his body that she loved. The shape of his head and neck, the line of his shoulders, the way his legs moved. Everything. Still, she could hardly breathe. "A *lot* more," he repeated.

Celie found the horse pretty impressive, all the same—a huge, Great Dane-sized, chestnut-colored, plush toy horse, with a black mane and tail, a padded fabric saddle and reins with fabric stars sewn onto them. "A gift for Carter?"

His goodbye gift, because Carter was going to Maine? The weight gone from Nick's shoulders—was that the weight of responsibility for the nephew he hadn't even known about until so recently? Some men would have been happy to shift the burden to a responsible family in a distant state.

"That's right," Nick answered. To the gift question, not to Celie's thoughts.

The horse was adorable, and Celie could so clearly imagine Carter as a toddler, treating it like a pet and a piece of gym equipment at the same time. It seemed important, somehow, that he should have gym equipment, the way Nick did. Big, soft, plush gym equipment, in place of Nick's chrome and steel and padded leather.

"What's happening, Nick?" she asked. "What have you and Ellen decided?" she asked. Nick didn't answer at once, so she added quickly, "I mean, I know that's none of my business, but—"

"We have to talk, Celie."

He pressed a button on his key fob, and the car gave an obedient squeak as the doors unlocked. He opened hers for her, and leaned on the top of it for a moment, looking at her with his heart-stopping blue eyes. Celie's breathing began to wobble even more. She wanted so much to share in the energy that seemed to radiate from her boss this afternoon, but an instinct for self-preservation held her back.

She'd already gotten herself hurt enough over him. She needed to build her barriers again, not have them knocked down by a mood in Nick that surely wouldn't last. Even if he was adopting Carter, and even though she'd be thrilled for both of them in that case, what did it have to do with her? Nick had shut her out of his personal life at all but the most desperate times. She didn't want to be his desperation measure, anymore.

"I want to get this in the right order, okay?" he said, his serious eyes still fixed on her face. "That seems real important, for some reason. Let's get to my place, first, before we talk."

"Okay."

He drove, frowning, and when she asked if anything was wrong, he just muttered, "I hope I haven't cut this too fine. I really wanted it to be perfect."

When they reached his house, he grabbed her hand as if he couldn't wait to get her inside, carrying the horse under his other arm. She noticed a second bit of paint on the garage's concrete step—a bright goldy-yellow, this time, instead of sky-blue, just one drop of it. Nothing else in the house looked different...

Until he'd pulled her upstairs, to his personal gym.

It wasn't his gym anymore.

All the black-and-silver gym equipment had gone.

It was Carter's room. Ready for Carter's equipment, instead.

Nick placed the big plush horse on the carpet and looked around. "The decorators finished a couple of hours ago," he said. "But the carpet seemed a little bare, so I went to the toy store and the horse just seemed to fit. Do you like it?"

"It's gorgeous, Nick." The words came out on a whoosh of breath. "It does fit."

"All of it, I mean. The whole room." He went to the windows and opened them up, to get rid of the smell of fresh paint. New drapes hung there, in colors that matched the murals on the walls. "I had the decorators use low-odor paint," he said. "But it's still pretty strong in here. I'd rather have the heat, if that's okay with you."

"It's fine. One of the vents in your office had gotten closed the other day, by the way. That's why it was so hot in there."

"Not important. Not today. Do you like the crib? The linen set?"

"I like all of it. It's all perfect."

She took in the meadow and sky murals in goldy-yellow and sky-blue and grass-green. She saw the matching painted shelves ready for books and toys. There were a few in place already, but not so many that Carter would be spoiled or overwhelmed. She saw a rocking chair, and a matching dresser set and crib, already made up with sheets and a quilt and coordinating bumper pads. She also saw the change table Nick had bought a few weeks ago.

"Did I get it in the right order?" he said. He strolled over to the tallboy and leaned his elbow on it, watching her. There were some little boxes sitting there. More toys?

"Um, I'm not—" She laughed, her stomach fluttery.

"No, okay, you don't understand yet, do you? Of course you don't."

"You're going to adopt Carter. I understand that, yes." The baby clearly wasn't here at the moment. "And I'm so happy about it. You must have known I would be."

"And you were the person who said what I needed to hear. Not Lisa in Maine. Not Ellen, trying her best to blackmail me emotionally with her daughter's offer. You. When you told me that all Carter needed was for me to *want* to be the best parent for him. And I remembered what Ellen herself said that very first day about a baby knowing who he's supposed to cling to. Do you remember?"

"I remember, yes."

"I realized I wanted him to cling to me, and that if I let Lisa and her husband adopt him and take him to Maine, he never would."

"No, you're right. He wouldn't."

"Or to you, Celie. He wouldn't ever cling to you. And that was just as important. Hell, *more* important. You were so right! I had to fit in what was important first. I had to want it. Just want it. And work out how to do it later. I discovered on Thursday that I wanted it. Today we have to start the working out.''

"Wait a minute! Wait!'' She pressed her hands to her head. "You're going way too fast for me, now, Nick! Carter wouldn't cling to me? You *want*... Carter...to cling...to me?''

Nick stepped closer and took her in his arms. "And I want to cling to you, too. See? Feel it? Feel me clinging?'' His voice dropped, almost to a whisper, and she felt the brush of his mouth on hers. She opened her eyes—when had she closed them?—and saw him looking into her face, frowning. "Did I get this in the right order? Now you have to tell me.''

"I—I don't know.'' She began to laugh, because his arms had tightened around her—warm, *wanted*— and now he was looking at her as if he'd just asked the most important question in the world and needed her answer. She told him, mocking herself a little, mocking her wildly racing heart, and the uncertainty she couldn't shake away. "Your objective wasn't as clearly outlined as usual, so I'm not sure if you've met your target or not. Ask the question so I can understand it, Nick.''

And so that I don't make the terrible mistake of assuming too much.

"I love you, Celie. I want to marry you.'' His lips brushed her mouth as he spoke. "I want to be Carter's father, and I want you to be his mom. It's a two-for-one offer, from the heart.''

"Two-for-one? Like a Delaney's dessert special?''

"One won't mean anything to me without the other. Carter and you. I need both of you.''

"Yes, oh, yes, Nick, so do I!'' Laughing and crying, she held him. "I didn't think it was ever going to be possible."

He pressed his forehead against hers, and his eyes clouded a little.

"I guess for a long time I needed the boxes and the boundaries that Mom and Dad encouraged Sam and me to put up," he said. "They helped, when we were kids. And they helped us to make Delaney's the success that we wanted it to be. But then I got to the point where I didn't know how to look beyond the boundaries, or how to blur them."

"Neither did I, at first," she confessed.

"You had a little mystic help."

"That didn't make it easier!"

"I guess not. But I couldn't see that at the time. Your dreams scared me. What they said and how they happened and all the rules they broke about the way we related to each other."

"It took me a while to feel comfortable with them, too," Celie said. "They pushed, and I resisted, and we both got angry and confused."

"Then we started to break the rules without any help from your dreams, and that was even worse. I kept thinking I'd do anything not to lose you as my assistant, even when I was angry with you for making it so clear that you thought I was handling all my decisions on Carter in the wrong way."

Celie looked up at Nick, so close. "Once I'd gotten involved in your personal life, I couldn't butt out, the way you wanted me to. It just didn't work that way. There was no turning back."

"We couldn't stay away from each other, but I'd only ever had the kind of relationships, before, that I knew would hurt you, and that weren't what you deserved. I couldn't see the whole picture clearly until Thursday, when Ellen called, and when you and I talked.''

"I thought you were going to decide that Carter would go to Maine. Then you just left, and I didn't know what was happening.''

"I rushed up to Cleveland and confronted Ellen with my ultimatum. I wasn't letting Carter go to Maine. But something was still missing, like a huge empty hole, and I realized it was you. Before I even knew about Carter, you and he were tied together, and when I knew what I wanted with Carter, it became crystal clear to me how much I wanted…loved…you. Is that possible, Celie? Tell me you'll marry me and make us a family.''

"I will. Oh, of course I will! I've felt this way for a long time, way before I knew it. When I did know it, it seemed impossible and scary, and I've been so tense. I love you, Nick. I love you, and I want to be your wife.''

He grinned, and the clouded look had gone from his eyes. "Which is convenient, really," he said, "because…have you looked at the top of the tallboy?''

"Um…'' She looked, and saw that row of little boxes, again. Twelve of them, all lined up, waiting for her to open them. She knew, now, what they would contain. They were ring boxes.

"I went a little crazy in the jewelry store this morning," Nick said. "Desperate for you to say yes to this.''

"I can say it again, if you want. Yes, Nick.''

"We'll return the ones you don't like. If you don't like any of them, we can go together and find something else.''

With Nick standing right behind her, holding her, Celie began to lift the hinged lids of the tiny boxes, and saw rubies and diamonds, emeralds and opals, sapphires and pearls.

"I can't do this now!" She laughed, her sense of helplessness new and strangely sweet. "You'll have to help me. Do you have a favorite?"

"All of them. That's why I couldn't choose," he said softly.

"You, too?"

"Me, too. Helpless. And for the first time in my life, it doesn't feel scary and wrong. I imagined each one of them on your hand, and in my head they all looked perfect. Just like you. My perfect Celie."

"Oh, Nick…"

She turned into his arms and he kissed her, long and sweet and slow.

They both heard the doorbell downstairs, minutes later. "Just at the right time," Nick said.

"You already know who it is?"

"It's Ellen, I hope. With Carter. This is working out exactly the way I wanted."

He grabbed her hand and they hurried downstairs. Ellen took one look at their faces and clapped her hands together, tears sparkling in her eyes.

"Oh, I knew it!" she said. "This is perfect! When I saw the picture of the two of you in the newspaper that day a couple of months ago, just something in the way you were standing, and the way you looked at her, Nick. I knew that if it could work out like this, it would be perfect!"

She kissed each of them, and Celie got tears in her eyes as well.

"Where's Carter?" Nick asked.

"Asleep in the car, with all the windows open. The trunk is crammed with his things. And a few of mine."

"You're staying over?" Nick asked. "Please do!"

"Figured you two might appreciate a baby-sitter tonight, if you have something to celebrate. It's up to you, of course."

"We definitely have something to celebrate." He smiled at Celie, and hugged her close once again. "We're getting married. Carter's going to have a mom and a dad."

They all heard a sad baby cry erupt from the back seat of Ellen's car, in the driveway, at that moment. "I guess he heard you," she said. "But he's got it wrong. He's supposed to think this is good news."

"Can I go to him?" Celie asked. "I want to pick him up and hug him and tell him it's the best news in the world."

She almost ran to the car, knowing that her husband-to-be was right behind her, and together they held their baby boy. And Carter must have guessed that something pretty good had just happened, after all, because he started beaming at them and flapping his little hands in excitement while the tears were still wet on his lashes.

"The mirror goes with the apartment," Celie told Kyla, six weeks later. "That's what I was told when I moved in. If you want it, that is."

"Oh, I want it," Kyla answered. Surrounded by the boxes she'd just brought up, she surveyed the apartment, now bare of all Celie's things. "It seems to belong, doesn't it?"

"I've always thought so."

"This place has such a good feeling about it. It's been great living at Mom's, while Nettie was little, but she's starting school this fall, so I don't need so much of Mom's time, and I wanted our own place. Nettie will have the little room for her bedroom, and we'll double up this big room as our living area and my bedroom. I'm so glad we fixed this up, because I've been looking in the newspaper for weeks and nothing that I saw felt right."

"Well, here are the keys, and I've written down a few details about the way things work."

"Don't worry, I'm not going to call you on your honeymoon with a question about lighting the oven. Do you need to get to your hair appointment? I can't believe the wedding is in six hours!"

"I'll see you there."

They gave each other a quick hug, and Celie left her old apartment for the last time as its legal tenant, wondering about that page of notes she'd typed up for Kyla. She'd mentioned the quirks of the washing machine and dryer in the basement, and the occasional tendency of the valves on the heating units to shut off on their own, but she'd said nothing about dreams, or dream stitchers, or the small, unexplainable items that could sometimes be found on the windowsill.

She smiled.

No problem.

If Kyla needed to know about any of that, she would find out when the time was right.

Celie's own dreams had tapered to nothing over the past three weeks. This might have been because she and Nick had been so busy rushing through the plans for their wedding, but at heart Celie wondered if it was because the Dream Stitcher didn't have anything important left to tell her.

Was that good? she wondered.

She had tried asking for some advice on which off-the-peg designer wedding dress to pick—she'd found two that she particularly loved—but even though the Dream Stitcher obviously knew a lot about beautiful gowns, she never offered an opinion.

In the street, Celie turned back for a last look at the old Victorian house, and under her breath she said a few words of thanks and farewell.

Veronica and her mom joined Celie at the hair salon, and then helped her dress in her cream satin gown back home in Mom's bedroom. When it came time to pin her veil, Celie brought out the Victorian hat pin she'd found on her windowsill—half a lifetime ago, it seemed.

"I want to use this, along with the other pins," she said. Something of the Dream Stitcher's, she added to herself, to make it seem as if she's here.

They arrived at the church right on time, at five o'clock, to be joined at the entrance by Veronica's husband, Alex, who would be escorting Celie down the aisle, with his wife as matron of honor. He had baby Lizzie in his arms and handed her over to his mother-in-law, who went ahead to take her place in the church. All the other guests were already assembled inside.

Having given themselves only six weeks to prepare, for the sake of securing Carter's future, Celie and Nick had chosen a simple occasion that would be more about celebrating family than creating the social event of the summer.

On her way down the aisle, Celie saw friends of

her own, and Rankin cousins, uncles and aunts. There were some strangers, too. Delaney family members, Celie guessed, as well as some of Ellen's sprawling clan. Nick's parents were here, too, of course, in the front row, but Marisa Delaney was nowhere in sight.

Also in the front row, she saw her mother with Lizzie, Ellen with Carter and Kyla and her mother with five-year-old Nettie. Right behind them stood Anna Jardine, her husband, Jack, and their little daughter. For a moment, through her veil, Celie thought she saw the silhouette of a woman, standing beside Anna, who looked faintly familiar. But then the fold in the veil moved, and she realized no one was there.

Then, just ahead of her, waiting near the altar, she saw the man of her heart—Nick, standing beside Sam.

"You look so beautiful," Nick whispered.

He took her hands in his and looked down in to her face, and in that moment, with her heart full to overflowing, Celie understood that she didn't need dreams and dream stitchers any more. She could see all that she needed to know about their future together, written in Nick's blue eyes.

* * * * *

Rediscover the remarkable O'Hurley family...

#1 *New York Times* bestselling author

NORA ROBERTS

BORN O'HURLEY

Starring her mesmerizing family of Irish performers in America.

The unique upbringing of the O'Hurley triplet sisters and their mysterious older brother has led to four extraordinary lives. This collector's-size edition showcases the stories of Abby and Maddy O'Hurley.

Available in August 2004.

Where love comes alive™

COMING NEXT MONTH

#1730 VIRGINIA'S GETTING HITCHED—
Carolyn Zane
The Brubaker Brides

Pragmatic Dr. Virginia Brubaker believed that compatibility—
not love—formed the basis of a lasting marriage. Ranch hand
Colt Bartlett couldn't resist that challenge, and so set out to
prove to the sassy psychologist that it was good old-fashioned
chemistry (and lots of kissing) that kept a marriage sizzling!

#1731 JUST BETWEEN FRIENDS—**Julianna Morris**

Spoiled little rich girl Kate Douglas may have been way out
of his league, but she was Dylan O'Rourke's best friend and
he'd do anything for her—even accept her temporary marriage
proposal so that she could inherit her grandmother's house.
But he never counted on Kate wanting the *man* more than the
mansion....

#1732 FALLING FOR PRINCE FEDERICO—
Nicole Burnham

Prince Federico diTalora always answered the call of duty…
to his sons and his kingdom. But when beautiful relief worker
Pia Renati came to stay at the palace, the only call he could
hear was the sudden beating of his heart!

#1733 BE MY BABY—**Holly Jacobs**

When an adorable baby was practically left on confirmed
bachelor Larry "Mac" Mackenzie's doorstep, his first instinct
was to run as fast as he could. But a little help from the thorny,
but seriously sexy Mia Gallagher might prove to this loner that
he was a family man after all....